TORTUROUS

GRIEF

By C.G. Buswell

Enjoy Scott's adventures!
Best wishes
Chris & Lynne

Also by C.G. Buswell

Novels

The Grey Lady Ghost of the Cambridge Military Hospital: Grey and Scarlet 1

The Drummer Boy: Grey and Scarlet 2

Buried in Grief

Short Stories

Christmas at Erskine

Halloween Treat

Angelic Gift

Burnt Vengeance

The Release

Christmas Presence

For you, dear reader, thank you for encouraging my writing and being part of my blossoming literary career.

Chapter One

Cameron stepped back into the shadows, satisfied that his route here had been unobserved. He had bided his time and performed recce after recce. There were no CCTV cameras here and none had detected his journey. More importantly, no cameras would monitor or record his trip to the cottage. He gave a wry smile despite the circumstances because he thought it ironic that a police station was just one street away. No vigilant homeowners had installed the ever-present all-seeing recording eyes, but then this was only a small town and not only were the police backwards, so too were the residents.

'No,' he thought, that's not fair at all, his mind must stop such dark thoughts, especially after tonight. He would do what he needed to do and then try and move on with his life after his duty was done. The people here had been such a support and he felt part of the community. As if in acknowledgment of his dark thoughts the door to a nearby pub opened and laughter swept onto the street as the bar staff said a cheerful goodnight to their favourite patrons who always stayed late for just one more drink. *'God, I could do with a drink myself,'* he thought.

'No!' he shouted inside his head. *'There is no God, no caring God would have allowed it to have happened, and no God will forgive me for what I am about to do.'* As if to affirm his commitment and take his mind off his wandering thoughts he snapped on his black latex gloves, the kind favoured by tattooists so as not to frighten their living canvases with

1

the sight of blood on normal coloured gloves. But this was not to be a normal night. Nor was he afraid of the sight of blood, in fact he relished it, much would be deservedly poured tonight. Blood did not revile him nor frighten him. He'd lost count of the times he had ran through blood, had it splash and seep up his boots, through his socks, soak up his trousers, penetrate through gloves, down through his wrists and squelch amongst his fingers and thumbs as he tried to save lives. Only tonight no lives would be spared.

A seagull silently swooped down through the alleyway on a carefully frequented route towards the kebab shop, conveniently placed between the pub and the nightclub. It knew that soon drunken revellers would be pouring out and dropping chips, lettuce and, if it was lucky, morsels of meat for it to devour. The bird knew it was worth the broken night's sleep and that his patience would pay off, as did Cameron as he waited silently and patiently for his target.

He had dressed in lightweight thermals to allow freedom of movement when the time came, and he was grateful for them as the temperature dropped on this harsh winter's night. But he had carefully chosen this time of year for he knew that most folk would be tucked up in bed or sat in front of the latest downloaded boxset munching on their snacks. There would be less people out and about and Cameron hoped for no witnesses. Not that being caught bothered him, he had so little to lose now, what he cherished had been so cruelly taken from him, and now, after months of training and careful planning he would even the balance sheet. He just needed a few hours, though days were preferable, if only he could.

He scratched at his nose through the black balaclava, its woollen fibres itching up though his nasal hairs. He started to control his breathing, the in and out mantra of slow breaths in through his nose and out through his mouth as the hypnotist had taught him. It helped to concentrate and focus his mind and slow down his heart rate. He could feel the balaclava become more sodden with each exhalation, but it was of no matter, soon his prey would be here, and Cameron would be on the move. He'd heard the bingo hall extractor fan switch off on the wall beside the sunken doorway, its whirling blades settling down to stillness as if it were a jet plane's engines coming to a steady halt after landing. His target was doing his rounds and had switched off the gent's toilet light.

Cameron had watched his quarry for months, there was no deviation, he was so rigid in his routine. He was the perfect prey. He would be with him in sixty seconds, time for his victim to set up the alarm, lock the doors and unsuspectingly walk down the alleyway to the rear car park. He had thought he'd got away with it, a year after his undetected crime, but Cameron was here to make him account for his sin.

Slowly Cameron took out his weapon from his pocket and unsheathed it, careful to put the cover safely back into his pocket. He carefully zipped it, moving slowly so as not to alert his approaching prey with any noise. He felt through his fabric, double checking that it was safely on his person. He wanted no evidence left behind. If he could, he had to be free for years to care for and support his wife.

3

The moon glinted off the weapon's sharpness, illuminating the determined evil intent in his eyes, before a cloud drifted across, plunging the alleyway back into darkness, for Cameron had used his skills with a catapult to shatter the glass and bulbs of the lampposts with carefully aimed stones. The local plod would blame it on kids in the morning, or perhaps in a few days' time, when some busybody reported the damage. He'd be long gone by then and so would his victim, though only his work friends from the bingo hall would miss him and Cameron had done his detective work and knew he'd be on his regular two days off.

Cameron smiled as the innocent and merry whistling grew louder. He knew that his prey was on his way and he mentally counted down to seven.

On the silently counted number one he grimaced with pleasure as he finished his breathing exercises by exhaling slowly through his mouth. His quarry walked past him, and Cameron broke the silence, stepped quickly out from the depths of the dark doorway, and said, 'David?'

The man, in his mid-thirties and dressed only in his black trousers, white shirt and blue bingo jacket, visibly startled with an instant jump, and quickly turned around and said, 'Aye? Who's...'

But his words fell short and froze in his vocal cords as Cameron reached out and grabbed his throat and with his momentum, carried him the two feet to the opposite wall, his victim's heels painfully dragging behind him. His target's back was slammed cruelly into the brickwork, causing pieces of weathered mortar to crumble to the pavement. His head stotted hard on the wall, but his attacker ignored the cries of unexpected and unwarranted pain coming from his prey and expertly moved his neck to the side to reveal the throbbing vein that was pumping adrenaline and blood through this man's shocked body. The needle was swiftly plunged into the prominent, pulsing vein and the syringe was depressed rapidly, delivering its payload within a millisecond. Perfectly executed by someone who had handled such equipment for years.

The man tried desperately to claw at his throat to take away this stranger's hands and what felt like a knife cutting into him. He became dizzy and disorientated, his thoughts were becoming jumbled, whirled, and confused, a needle perhaps? Hot liquid was swirling inside his neck and danced with his blood, embraced in a melody of warmth as it writhed and infused whilst making its way to his brain. Then the muddled questions started. *Why was this man hurting him, why was he dressed all in black? Who was he, why was he now putting his arm around my shoulder? What does any of it matter? I'll just let him walk me back to my car, that's it, I'll go with him, I'm sure I'll be safe with him…*

Chapter Two

It never surprised Cameron just how heavy a human body could be. David was now in a deeply relaxed and suggestive state; thanks to the black-market drug he'd just pumped into his vein. He didn't want to risk a needle-stick injury, this vile monster probably had all sorts of diseases, so he was doing this one handed, just his left arm supporting the evil man. His right was busy keeping a firm grip on the syringe, needle pointed outwards like a knight's lance. Though Cameron had started on a journey that was far from chivalrous. 'There's a good lad,' he said soothingly, though his eyes said differently, 'you come with me and I'll see you safely to bed where you can have a good long sleep.'

David gave an incoherent mumble but allowed himself to be led by Cameron down the dark alley, his feet scraping on the path, ruining his favourite black brogues. But it did not worry him, nothing concerned him, he was floating in a chemical fugue of apathy that dissipated indifference throughout his mind and body. He smiled as they neared the car park and he saw his car, his pride and joy, gleaming in the moonlight, though there were seagull droppings smeared down from the roof and driver's window like an offensive offering from the sky Gods. 'Oh well,' he thought, *it really doesn't matter, it'll wash off, nothing really matters, not anymore. I'll just do as this nice man wants me to do.'*

Cameron cursed under his breath as he heard the giggling. He quickly pulled the balaclava from his head, careful not to stab himself with the needle, which he dropped into the open garment and then wrapped its fabric around the syringe. He quickly transferred it to his other hand and now used both arms to support the drug-addled David. He faked a smile and a laugh as he neared the source of the giggling, two inebriated teenagers enjoying each other's company against a wall. They looked too engrossed in each other to take any notice of Cameron, but he didn't want to take any chances. A drunk couple probably wouldn't remember his face but may recall a balaclava-clad man carrying off a staggering bloke.

As he passed them, he gave them a cheeky wink and patted David's drooping head with his now free right hand and said, 'Craig's had too much to drink tonight. I'm just seeing him safely home. It looks like you two are having fun.' For effect he pretended an overjoyed chuckle, though he knew tonight was no laughing matter.

The young lad did not even bother turning around but continued trying to lift the short skirt of his companion. He waved at Cameron with his free hand, as if shooing him away. His lips were busy smooching into his potential lover's neck. Cameron smiled at the contrast of sensations between this and what he'd done moments ago. This couple were no threat, they only had eyes for each other. He made his way to the edge of the car park, towards the dimly lit part of it.

The teenage girl was too busy warding off the lad's fumbling hands, whilst giggling encouragingly and contradicting her comments of, 'not here, let's go somewhere more private.'

'In a minute love, this is too nice, besides they have gone now,' he broke away from her neck and kissed her full on the mouth and was over-joyed when he felt her probing tongue and reciprocated lips press hard on his as she reached down and started to furiously unbuckle his belt.

Cameron carefully sat David into his passenger car seat, even taking the trouble to put his seat belt on for him. He couldn't care less if he had to stop the car suddenly and he went through the windscreen, he just didn't want to be stopped by a vigilant police-officer on route to the cottage. He grabbed David's lopping head and banged it down to the headrest to give the impression to any observant passer-by that David was sleeping off a good night's bevy. He closed the door and quickly walked around to the driver's seat. Over by the other side of the car park he could make out the snogging couple, they were completely oblivious to him, wrapped up in each other's bodies for warmth and comfort.

Once in the car he put on some leather gloves to disguise his black latex gloves so that his hands on the steering wheel would not arouse any suspicions. He looked across to David, his pencil thin moustache reminded Cameron of a silent film actor. He knew that this man was no screen hero and as his head flopped down once more Cameron reached across and roughly pushed it against the passenger window. It gave a satisfying thump as his head struck the reinforced glass, bounced once and then sat there at an angle; just another drunken passenger fallen asleep on the drive home. Cameron started the engine and obliged by taking this man to his final resting place.

Chapter Three

David awoke with a start and tried to sit up. He strained against the thick green cords that were bound across his chest and legs. There was no give in them, no matter how much he struggled. He looked down and as his vision started to clear he could see that his legs were bound to plain wooden chair legs. Despite his grogginess, he knew that his chest must be bound to the chair too, but he struggled, nonetheless.

'I wouldn't bother,' mocked a voice that he didn't recognise, but did seem distantly familiar. 'The Scouts taught me how to tie knots and the Army taught me how to bind a man. You aren't getting away.'

As if to confirm this fact, David tried once more, but to no avail. Now that this sudden fright had expelled the drug from his bloodstream thanks to his heightened fear, he could now see that his hands were on his lap. He tried to grab out to the man, but his hands and fingers would not move.

'Plasticuffs. Your tainted fingers and hands are going nowhere sunshine. The Special Forces use them all the time. They taught me so much.'

David now looked up and was shocked to see a muscular figure standing confidently, legs akimbo, about two feet away, arms across his chest. This served to heighten the effect of his musculature. What frightened him the most was the black balaclava and its narrow slits for eyes. There were no such slits for the nose or mouth. But the eyes said it all, *'I'm in command and soon you will suffer.'* He could feel his bowels weaken.

As if sensing his fear Cameron took a step forward, bent down and put his face in front of David's. He looked deep into his eyes, as if searching into his soul, judging him, and deciding. 'Don't worry, I'm used to all sorts of shit. I was an army nurse. Take a good look around you, do you know where you are?'

Now that his vision was clearer and the effects of the forcefully injected drug had worn off, David could see much clearer. He looked around at the tarpaulin and plastic covered floor. 'HELP!' he shouted, 'SOMEONE HELP ME!'

Cameron laughed, 'Make as much noise as you want sunshine, take a good look at the walls and ceiling.'

David was startled into quietness by the surprisingly calm nature of the man. As he looked around him, he could see why. Glued to all the walls and even the ceiling and the backs of the door were what looked like black foamed egg cartons.

'That's right, I've soundproofed. Listen,' and with that he pushed his face right into David's and let out the loudest and basest animalistic roar imaginable. David strained backwards on his restraints but could not escape the frightening noise that caused his bladder to spasm and pour out its warm contents throughout his lap and down his trousers. The man stood upright and took a small step back as if escaping the flow of the urine.

The man laughed, 'but that's not why the tarps and plastic are there,' he took out a metal object from his pocket and David heard a sharp click. 'This is why,' and with a swoosh of a flick-blade he sliced deeply across David's trousers at his thigh.

'Aaaggh,' screamed David as he felt the sharp blade slice through fabric and then his skin, muscle, and fat in an instant. Dizzy spasms overwhelmed him as he fought to contain the pain that washed over him in torrents of swells as his blood pushed through white fatty layers, bubbled up and poured over his skin and hit the floor with a splash, followed by a steady flow.

'Now you know why the plastic is here.' Cameron took a step forward and leaned down to the man's ear and whispered, 'but you won't bleed out just yet, not for a long time, I have to do unmentionable things to you. I promised them and myself.'

David shuddered, not at the pain, but at the whispered comment, 'HELP!' he continued to shout between waves of pain. 'FOR GOD'S SAKE, SOMEONE HELP ME!'

Cameron used the back of his hand to whip across David's mouth, to shut him up. 'No-one will hear you, so shut up. I need to talk to you, to make you understand, do you hear me?'

Despite himself a shocked David nodded furiously, his phlegm and spittle went flying across the room, as if reaching out for help, with each desperate nod.

'Good,' said Cameron as he reached across to the nearby table and opened a green canvas bag. 'Like I said, I was an army nurse, a bloody good one too, saved a lot of lives, even worked with the

Special Forces during their training. They train with live ammunition, so combat medics, nurses and doctors are always on stand-by.' He reached into the holdall and withdrew a padded plastic pouch and tore it open. 'I'm going to save your life, for the moment,' he cautioned as he took out a bulky bandage and brutally pressed it down on David's bleeding thigh. Now it was his turn to roar, in abject pain as Cameron continued to press down deliberately, not just to stop the man from bleeding. 'I stemmed the flow of blood, hurts, doesn't it?'

David nodded furiously, eyes wide open, no longer confused, he now knew where he was and who this was.

Cameron diligently wrapped the bandage tight around the open wound, ignoring the flow of blood that oozed out. 'It'll stop in a moment. I've seen better men than you take the pain, and their wounds were worse. Fragment grenades and bullets do some awful damage. Ah!' he exclaimed as he looked up to see David looking around him properly. 'I see you recognise the place. You should, it was here, wasn't it? So now you know who I am.'

Once again came the furious nodding, as if agreeing would see his bonds released.

'Good, now I can take this off.' Cameron carefully moved around the slippery blood and stood in front of David, immune to the stench coming from him. He bent down so that they were face to face and slowly peeled off his balaclava. He pulled it off from above his scalp so that it came slowly away, revealing his facial features bit by bit like a macabre striptease.

13

David neither found it alluring or enthralling, but he was captivated nonetheless, he slowly saw an older version of his former friend before his eyes. The jaw was muscular, but starting to sag, there were wrinkles around the mouth and bags under the eyes, the same piercing blue eyes that entranced you and drew you in, and finally the same hair, but speckled with grey. 'You are Fra…'

'NO!' shouted Cameron as he punched David full on the face, 'No! You don't get to say that, you are not worthy, you are just a piece of shit, a piece of meat. You are an animal that I have to put down and butcher.' As if to confirm his thoughts he reached across, stretched out David's left ear and with another expert flick of the blade, cut it clean off.

David howled, an animalistic base sound, deep from his ancestral past as Cameron macabrely laughed. 'You see, this is what you have made me. I was once a gentle person, wanting to heal, to help people. But your actions last year unsettled my mind. You have entered my nightmares and deeply troubled my soul and my thoughts. I have become this because of you. I sought out the brave soldiers I treated and each willingly trained me in their specialist skills after they heard my story over a few beers. It was Dave who taught me knife skills, Brian the Intelligence bod taught me how to observe you over months of reconnaissance and John taught me interrogation techniques that will have you kneeling on the floor begging for mercy.'

Cameron walked around David, still ignoring his cries of pain. He stooped down to his other ear and whispered, 'but guess what, I'll be showing you no mercy.'

David's cries stopped abruptly as Cameron slowly walked back around to face him. He stooped down once more so that they were eye to eye and he slowly and menacingly whispered, 'you won't be getting out alive for what you did.'

David struggled helplessly against his bonds and screamed out, 'You Monster!'

Cameron head-butted David furiously and regained his balance and with it his composure, he was immune to the pain in his head, his emotions over-riding all sensations, he was so engrossed to his mission. 'NO! You are the monster and like all evil things you must be destroyed.' He walked across to the medical kitbag once more and took out a large black bag. He unpacked it as he walked across to the plastic covered sofa and then unfurled it across its length. 'Do you know what this is dickhead?'

David's eyes widened and his fear reached a dizzyingly new level, he knew perfectly well what it was, he'd seen them on television.

'That's right sunshine, I've sadly had to put a few brave men and women into them over the years. Or what was left of them.' He casually threw in the ear and it bounced across the unzipped body bag before laying down appropriately at the head end of the heavy-duty plastic. 'You, or what's left of you, is going in there. But don't worry, one of the lads now runs a crematorium, so you'll get taken care of, in the dead of night and with no mourners. I doubt you'd have had

15

any, you don't go around making friends do you, your evil. You just destroy lives. But look at me again, swearing my bloody head off. I never swore either, until you came into our lives and robbed us of happiness. Now I have so much anger that no amount of counselling or psychotherapy will cure it, though I've tried.' Cameron stopped talking and bounced the knife's flat edge a few times on his palm, as if deep in thought. He then pointed it directly at the quivering David, 'but you will. Once I'm finished with you, I know my anger will be all spent, as will you.'

'Help,' trembled David as his shouting subdued as he fought his pain and fear. His voice was quieter, as if almost resigning himself to his fate.

Cameron chuckled as he pointed his arms around the room, 'did I forget to mention that there is acoustic plasterboard under the soundproofing sheets. It took me months, but it was worth it. I come in here to scream my head off at the injustice of it all, bloody Police, can't trust them to do a thorough job. Not enough evidence for a prosecution. Oh, they know all about you sunshine, they just can't make it stick.' Cameron looked down and sardonically grinned, 'not like your blood, eh, it's sticking a treat to the plastic, drying off nicely, you must have good clotting factors. It's a shame you won't be around to donate blood, the transfusion service would love a pint or two from you. Do you donate?'

A surprised David shook his head, trying desperately to appease the man.

'No, I didn't think a selfish prick like you would,' he then casually walked across to the other table and heaved it across so that it was in eyesight of David. He then nonchalantly withdrew a long wooden handle from a large black holdall and playfully left the other end unrevealed in the bag. He then glanced at David's bound legs, looked him in the eye with a stare that could freeze blood, and quickly grasped the handle and withdrew the object, swung it at David and cleanly chopped through his ankle.

David roared in devastating pain, then shuddered and drooped forward, unconscious with shock, oblivious to his blood pumping out across the room and down onto the floor.

Cameron wasted no time watching the squirting liquid. He dropped the axe and leapt to the other table and from his medi-bag withdrew a tourniquet and expertly applied it just below the knee of the brutally amputated foot. 'There you go sunshine, that'll keep you going for a bit longer.' He looked up and wasn't surprised to see that he had collapsed with shock. 'Now you know why I bound you so tightly to the chair, the interrogator taught me that. It saves a lot of picking up and carrying.' He stooped down and picked up the bloody foot by the protruding, cleanly shorn bones, again not surprised at the weight of a single foot and ankle. He held it up, as if appraising its quality, and then whacked David across the cheek with his own shoe and foot. 'C'mon, wake up sunshine, I do have all night, but I don't want to keep Billy at the Crem waiting. He's all fired up to meet you!' He laughed as he dropped the foot.

The sick joke was lost on David who was mumbling incoherently but soon came to with a few more slaps around the face, this time with the now bloodied pulp end of his ankle. He screamed and screamed until Cameron stuffed an unfurled bandage into his mouth.

'It's not that I mind the screams, Christ but I've heard some wounded screams in my time, but I'd like you to try and calm down.'

In defiance David violently shook his head and tried to spit out the bandage, but to no avail. He soon stopped when he saw Cameron pick up the axe again.

'That's better,' said Cameron in a surprisingly soothing voice as he put the bloodied axe back into the bag. He then walked back to David and picked up his amputated foot, scuffed shoe still intact. He raised it to David's eyeline and threw it across to the body bag. It landed with a soft thud, the sofa absorbing the impact in the spot that Cameron had carefully aimed, at the foot, near to the start of the zip. 'Howz about that then?' he said, not expecting any praise from David. 'Now, I just need your attention for a moment longer. You see I don't need your forgiveness, nor will you plead for any from me. It'll fall on deaf ears.' Cameron couldn't help but look quickly behind him at the body bag as he made this inadvertent gag. 'You see I just want to kill you, slowly. But I must be home before my wife misses me, she's my alibi. I gave her extra sleeping tablets, so she's fast asleep now. In the morning, she will wake up and find me beside her and she'll swear to anyone that asks that I was by her side all night. To her it will seem like she is telling the truth, so I'll not be making her tell a lie. You see, we are a nice law-abiding family, lies don't come easy to us, but killing now does to me. So, allowing for Billy to incinerate you before his colleagues come to work, I reckon I've about an hour. I shan't ask where you'd like your ashes scattered as you're going down the toilet, that's all you deserve. I just hope you don't block the Crematorium toilets. But Billy will be going from ladies to gents like a tourist after a Spanish paella and spread you out between flushes. He's got the bone-crusher looked out, so no worries there. I just need you to know that I know it was you and that I don't forgive you, nor does my wife and daughter. You've devastated our lives and now it's time to end your life so that you don't do this to anyone else.' Cameron looked across to the medi-bag and nodded to it, 'I could have kept you alive for days, and in agony, with the contents of that bag, but instead I'll have fun with the contents of the other bag.' He nodded to the other table.

Eyes wide open and anxiety-ridden sweat pouring from every pore, despite the winter chills, David couldn't help but watch Cameron as he carefully walked around the drying blood on the floor and opened the bag. 'It's a torturers holdall, full of implements to get information from suspects, fast and cleanly.' He picked up a small metal probe and held it to the light glowing down from the ceiling lightbulb. 'The nervous system is so fascinating, so delicate too. This small thing can delve deep, leave so little scarring, but it can do so much internal damage and cause so much pain. Please, indulge me.' Cameron then swiftly reached across to David, pulled out the bandage from his mouth, grabbed his jaw and thrust the probe through his chin and deep into his skin and beyond.

The scream that erupted from David was beyond anything on this earth that Cameron had heard. Even the most wounded of soldier had not uttered such cries. But sadly, he took no pleasure, no emotion was on his face, his eyes contained such sorrow that could never be healed as he twisted and poked the probe as if seeking solace from his grief. He pulled it out as quickly as it had entered and then grabbed David's jaw and pulled it up so that he was facing him. He looked down with such venom and hatred, drew back his hand and punched and punched until his black latex gloves had split open and his blood was mingling with his victim's.

Chapter Four

The phone rang and vibrated in Cameron's pocket and stopped him in his rhythmic punching of the bloodied mushy pulp that was David. Cameron stepped back, broken teeth crunching underfoot, exhaustion threatened to overcome him, and he looked at his victim's face, which was now beyond recognition, but still intact enough to allow him to breathe, but only just as he rasped out between broken teeth and oozing blood and mucus.

He ignored his bloodied victim and grabbed for a towel from the kitbag and quickly wiped his hands before delving into his trouser pocket for his phone.

'It's toasty warm here mate!' exclaimed Billy in code, sensitive to anyone listening into his call. 'Will you be around in an hour?'

'No bother, I'll bring the bread,' replied Cameron, 'it's all but wrapped up.'

Billy hung up, Cameron not bothered by the abruptness of the call being terminated, it was how they were trained. Besides, he needed to do more to David.

He put away his phone and walked over to behind David and switched on a socket.

David straining to hear, imagining all sorts of strange fresh horrors. He heard a gurgle of water and the rattle of steam erupting from a metal device. *'Surely the sicko isn't making a cup of tea?'* he randomly thought between waves of pain before falling unconscious again.

Cameron walked back around the chair and reached into the medi-bag and pulled out more latex gloves, the normal fleshy coloured ones this time. He then reached forward and grabbed David's chin, or what was left of its ravaged skin and bone. He inadvertently pushed his finger through and into the jaw. This awakened David with a scream of fresh torturous pain. Cameron ignored him and let go of his chin and walked over to the other bag and pulled out what looked like stainless-steel pliers, though these had sharp edges. He walked slowly to David and gently took his hands.

David tried to resist but the plasticuffs held him tight and Cameron was slowly unfurling his fingers for him. He was just on the edge of being numb from his bindings. He watched in morbid fascination as to what was going to happen whilst being totally petrified. He had no more bodily fluids to evacuate in his fear.

'You see, there is just me doing this, and I have to get you, or rather what's left of you, into the boot of the car.' He pointed to the body bag with the stainless-steel tool, 'I've a few more of those, so I thought a third of you in each one, to distribute the weight, you know?' Cameron didn't wait for an answer and closed the tool down on the index finger of David, near to the knuckle and pushed down with all his might. There was a soft crunch and then a sharp crack and the finger came loose, Cameron quickly stepped aside as David vomited as floods of fresh pain crashed through his body and overpowered him. Cameron then stepped back, quickly but cleanly cut off David's remaining digits and then reached behind David's chair for the now heated cordless iron and thumped it against the bleeding knuckles and cauterised the wounds. He didn't want to have to do too much cleaning before the morning. He'd hoped to just pick up the tarps and sheets and have them burnt with the body parts.

The air filled with the acrid stench of burning flesh, like at an inventive barbeque for cannibals. All that was needed was some lip-smacking tasty sauce. The smell was heightened by the vehement chugging of the steam from the iron as it released its vapours into the room. Cameron drolly wondered at the humour of the emergency services and armed forces and how many, like him, could see and smell such sights and then go home and cook a meal or munch on a takeaway or ration pack. He picked up the fingers, thinking that if he had time, how much fun it would be to get a blender from the kitchen and liquefy the fingers and thumbs in front of David. But he was no monster, a monster would make him drink the contents. In his darkest of nights since this monster came into their lives he had imagined doing all sorts of ghoulish things to David, but now time was of the essence, he had to finish him off, distribute him in the body bags, clean up, drop off the remains to Billy, get home, wash up and lay with Karina before she woke up.

'Please, please let me go,' croaked David as teeth and blood dropped from his mouth. 'I won't tell anyone, please take me to a hospital.'

'It's a wee bit too late for that laddie,' laughed Cameron holding on to the slippery digits, 'besides, you've your own private

23

nurse here.' He walked over to the body bag and almost reverently placed them in the middle of the black plastic. He walked back to the interrogator's bag and took out a scalpel and what looked like heavy duty bolt-cutters. 'Aye. It's far too late for a hospital and you will be by-passing the morgue and undertakers, besides, I've seen too much of them lately, thanks to you. Now, if you believe in God, say a prayer, because I'm about to send you to Hell, where you belong.' He advanced upon David with the scalpel outstretched.

'OH, GOD, NO, SWEET JESUS, WHAT ARE YOU DOING NEXT YOU MADMAN?' screamed David.

'Not quite the prayer I would have chosen,' he replied as he squatted down and placed the bolt-cutter like tool on David's wet lap.

David tried to squirm and started to scream out for help. But the restraints held him firm and fast and the soundproofing absorbed all the noise as nothing stirred outside the cottage. Even the owl in the tree was not hooting tonight but sat perched rotating its head around as if in vigilant guard against intruders coming to disturb Cameron and his duty.

'Sh, sh,' cajoled Cameron, to get David's attention. 'I need you to listen now,' he said as he clamped his free hand over David's mouth. 'You broke our hearts. I promised myself that one day I would rip your heart out for what you did. And today that day has come.' He reached into his pocket and took out a photograph and held it in front of David's eyes. He allowed David to stare at it for a few more moments and then he carefully put it back into his pocket.

24

There was no longer any struggling from David, he dropped his head down and sighed, as if resigning himself to his fate. He was beyond pain now, or rather thought he was until he felt Cameron cut deeply into his chest with the ultra-sharp scalpel. He tried to sit upright, to back away from the pain, but his bindings held him securely, he arched his head up as if trying to reach to the heavens and gave the most guttural of screams as Cameron threw the scalpel aside and used the other larger tool to crunch and separate his ribs.

Cameron ignored the howling coming from his victim and reached into his chest cavity, blood pouring out and onto the sheeting, soaking though to the tarpaulin, flowing around the floor seeking out a nook to fill. He held his victim firmly by the shoulders and used his elbow to position his face to within a millimetre of his and breathed calmly before he said, 'I promised myself that I would look you in the eye as I tore your heart out just like you've wrenched out theirs and mine.' He grasped the rapidly beating organ, surprised at its warmth, then placed his right foot onto David's lap and used all his force to pull backwards, shrieking into the monster's face as he wrenched it from his body. They screamed in unison like two lovers climaxing simultaneously until with one final anguished twist Cameron broke their bonding and pulled out the life-affirming organ that briefly pumped and then was as still as the bloodied body slumped in the chair.

Chapter Five

The gate gave its signature squeak as it was opened, and the gravel grumbled underfoot as Cameron made his way slowly up the path. As always, he ignored those to the left and right and he turned off as he reached the cast-iron bench where so many, like him, had sat alone and openly wept in their helplessness and despair.

He walked up the well-worn grass path and stopped and touched the black granite stone and stroked the ears of the family dog who was engraved opposite the white dove in flight. He thought, as he always did, that if there was a heaven, and he hoped that there was, that it was guiding his spirit heavenwards.

Despite his aching knees, he kneeled on the sunken grass which was undulated along six feet and three feet across. He sighed in pain and despair as his hands reached out and touched the gilded lettering on the headstone that spelt out his son's name.

'And that's what I should have done Fraser, I should have tortured to death the man that was responsible for your death. And I would have too if I hadn't made a promise to your mum. She needs me, more than ever now son. Her illness is getting worse and she needs more help around the house. She tells me that she wouldn't know what she'd do without me. I must do more and more for her, help her dress, shower, and get onto the toilet. I promised her that I'd be there for her, and for your sister, and that I wouldn't pursue him and end up in jail. I can't take care of them both from a prison cell.

As much as I love and miss you, I know I have to obey the law and do what is right.' Cameron reached down to the dipped grass and placed his palm there, as if trying to reach down through the earth and into the coffin to hold his son's hand one more time.

'But God knows, I'd rip him apart if I could. I'd make him pay for what he did to you.' Tears dropped from his eyes, ran down his nose and onto the grass, helping to rejuvenate fresh growth amongst the blades and the moss, only this water from the living would not bring him back.

Author's Note

Please forgive this brutal story. Now and then, us writers feel the burning need to put down on paper the emotions we feel through a story or novel, please excuse such indulgences on my part as I work through some issues before bringing you more uplifting stories. My dark side needs a bit more exploring, and I think with one or two more novels my writing skills should be more colourful and happier once more. Scott, from the Grey and Scarlet series, deserves a bit of happiness and one day, perhaps, I shall be in a better place to share him with you once more, or so my therapist tells me!

If you liked this short story, then please leave a review at Amazon.co.uk or GoodReads.com and even on my Facebook page at facebook.com/cgbuswell and twitter.com/CGBUSWELL

Thank you, dear reader.

Chris

www.cgbuswell.com

Acknowledgements

Thank you, 'Padre' Katherine and Ray Hyman of Cruden Bay IT Services, www.crudenbaytraining.co.uk for the proof-reading and spotting my whopping errors so that my dear readers can read me at my best.

Amanda, at Let's Get Booked, has done a marvellous job on the cover. Thank you. See more of her covers at www.letsgetbooked.com where you might find a new indie and traditionally published author to read. But first, read on, there are some previously published short stories of mine to read as a bonus. The first is a stand-alone horror story. This is then followed by several from the Grey and Scarlet series which take place between and after The Grey Lady Ghost of the Cambridge Military Hospital and The Drummer Boy novels.

Burnt Vengeance

By C.G. Buswell

Andrew listened to the laboured breathing of his best friend, hoping that each would be his last. He wanted his friend to die in peace and to pass away quickly. He hated seeing his pal of thirty years struggle on, gasping for breath like a landed fish floundering helplessly and clinging on desperately for life. Yet he inhaled again, that raspy, deep chested, rattling sound that was overheard above and in sharp contrast to the gentle and constant sound of the oxygen piped through from the wall behind David's bed. Andrew shivered involuntarily, he had come to loathe both sounds and knew that when he came to rest his head next to his girlfriend again tonight that he would hear all these sounds in his sleep, as if his chum had come to rest by them.

It had worsened with each daily visit, as if David were morbidly rattling some chain links attached to his bed. He looked drained of blood. He had the grey pallor of the dying, the shade that made people take a startled step backwards upon first seeing the person. Until shame and relief that it was not them caught up with the viewer. Andrew didn't want to reach out and take the weak, cold, clammy hand of his life-long friend, but forced himself to hold it. He had to appear normal to his dying friend, despite his sins. He silently judged himself and found himself guilty. It ate into his soul, crumbling his consciousness with each bite, devouring his humanity like a tasty morsel.

David felt the loose, comforting double tap on his hand, a habit his chum had developed over the last few days, just before

32

holding his hand in friendship, as if already saying goodbye. David returned the handhold by first two gentle, but weak taps before gripping Andrew tightly, or as tight as he could in his cancer ridden weakness.

'Promise me again,' cried out David in despair before a wracking coughing fit engulfed him as he forced vital air out of his eaten-away lungs.

As always, he secretly cursed his chum for introducing the habit of smoking after their Friday night Boy's Brigade fun. He'd sneaked two cigarettes from his father's packet, along with a small box of matches from his mum's knick-knack drawer that everyone has in their kitchen. Andrew had wanted to share this new experience, like all new experiences throughout their lives, together. In unison, they had taken a long draw of the cigarette, thinking that they were cool. All illusions of looking suave and mature for their young age were swiftly shattered as they bent over coughing, gasping for a lungful of fresh clean air, as if they were two old men in a chest unit of a hospital. But it had not stopped them trying them again and again until both became twenty a day addicted men.

David was glad that his friend had not developed lung cancer like he had. Andrew had the greater inner strength of the two and one day had decided to stop smoking in his early twenties. David, as always, admired the resolve of his friend and wished that he could have done so as well. No matter though, he had loved this man's company for over thirty-five years. He would be glad of his lifetime of friendship until he took his dying breath, which he knew would be any day now. As he struggled to catch his breath, he reached for his oxygen mask and tried to take in its life-saving gases, knowing that this was only prolonging the inevitable. He flailed his free arm helplessly in the air.

Andrew recognised the sign and took his hand gently from the grip of David and reached for a tissue and placed it in David's hand, careful not to get snagged onto the intravenous tubing that pumped in his morphine at a steady rate to keep his best friend as pain free as possible. With his other hand, he reached out and took the oxygen mask from his friend's withering hand, his finger bones were prominent in folds of skin, protruding out like skeletal talons on a re-animated corpse. It would not be long, he thought selfishly, and soon David would die and he could get on with his life with her. Guilt swept over him and engulfed him like a tsunami hitting a beach, threatening to wash him violently away in its wake. He must stop this dark train of thought as he knew that love must conquer, what started as lust had blossomed into mutual love and no-one must take this chance of happiness away from him. He swayed his guilt over Sandra by concentrating on the job at hand as he held the oxygen mask away from his friend's face so that he could spit into the tissue the dark bilious matter that he coughed up from the depths of his stomach and lungs. In a well-drilled movement, he replaced the mask and took the soiled tissue, absently folded it, as if not wanting to see physical evidence of the cancer he knew he was responsible for, and popped it into the bin by the sink.

'Try and stay calm David, concentrate on taking a few deep breaths like the nurses here told you, then you'll soon get better.'

David started his raspy coughing again, only this time there was nothing to cough up and he didn't need his oxygen mask moving away. Instead he clung to it like a shipwrecked sailor to some drifting flotsam, hanging grimly for dear life. His coughing developed into laughter.

'Take a good look around you Andrew, I'm in a hospice. They don't send you here to get better. The nurses are doing a great job, but we both know that I'm on my way out.'

'Some do, you know that, you've been in and out here a few times. The staff nursed you better, well enough to go home. Maybe you'll get home soon.'

David's laughter grew deeper and throatier, the cackle of a life-long smoker that only stopped when the coughing started again and took over.

Andrew sat patiently waiting for the coughing to subside, it took several minutes, the silence, but for the distressing hacking, became a huge gulf between the friends.

'No, mate,' David finally wheezed out, 'I'm dying, and this is my final visit to the hospice.'

'Yes, I know mate,' replied Andrew once again doing the double tap with his hands, only this time it was on David's shoulder. He didn't know if he did this to make himself or his friend feel better. 'I just feel so helpless. I love you man.'

'Don't get all soppy, we both know that I'll be dead in a few days,' wheezed out David.

Andrew waited for his pal to catch his breath once more. The last few days had taught him to patiently wait for his pal to finish his sentences.

'Just promise me...'

This time Andrew interrupted him because he knew what was coming and wanted to save his pal from the effort. 'I know mate. I'm to make sure you get cremated. We've been over this countless times. I understand why you don't want to be buried, ever since that potholing accident we had. But we survived.'

David's eyes widened and he struggled to try and sit further up from the propped-up pillows. He re-gripped his friend's hand. If anything, it was tighter this time, as if to give further emphasis to his words.

'PROMISE ME!' he shouted, before collapsing back into the softness of the pillows as a further coughing fit played itself out.

'You know I will. I won't let anyone bury you again. I'll make sure you go to the crematorium.'

'And, the, rest?' wheezed out David, before sagging back into the pillows.

'Oh man, I've never let you down before, but I don't know how I can do it. Those places have strict guidelines and protocols. Everything will be locked down.' He looked into his friend's eyes; they were wide like a startled rabbit in the headlights. 'Please don't make me feel guiltier than I already am, I should never have offered you that cigarette, all those years ago, filthy things. If you hadn't had kept smoking, you'd never have been here in the first place. Instead we could have been hanging off a cliff, trying to be the first up so as not to have to get the first beers in.'

David tried to smile through his fear, grateful for his friend's presence here. 'Just promise me that one thing,' he croaked out with great effort.

'Okay, I promise you David that I will make sure that I am there when the undertakers screw closed your coffin.'

'And…' encouraged David.

'And that somehow, I will find a way to be there whilst you are cremated, though goodness knows how I'll manage it.'

David inhaled deeply, preparing himself for important words that he did not want marred by another coughing fit. 'Oh, you'll find a way mate, you always do, you always get what you want, don't you?'

Sandra cupped Andrew's face in her hands and drew closer for a kiss. He bobbed his head back, evading her lips.

'Stop feeling so guilty,' she said, 'it's you I love. It won't be too long now. I think he'll only last a day or two.'

He reluctantly took her hands from his face, luxuriating in their soft warmth. 'But you are his girlfriend,' he sighed, heavy with remorse.

She gripped his hands, pumping them up and down several times, as if emphasising what she was about to say and wanting him to agree, 'And I'll continue to be his girlfriend until he dies, but then my heart will be with you, where it has always been.'

37

'It's so bad love, I've been sleeping with you whilst he's been dying, and it was me that got him hooked on those damned cigarettes in the first place. What am I supposed to do?'

'You keep visiting him. You keep loving him, like I still do. We can't help what happened, falling in love, making love, it's just natural. I needed comfort when he was first ill in hospital and you gave me what I needed. Better you than some uncaring stranger from Tinder.'

'I feel like I took advantage of you,' sighed Andrew.

'No, my love, no. We were on the cards for years. Every time you came around my heart would be aflutter, we were like two beautiful white doves ready to mate, it was you who I thought about all the time. Don't you deny it either, I saw it in your eyes. You were mentally undressing me whenever David wasn't looking. It doesn't mean that I love David less, but why deny ourselves happiness. You are single, so no-one is getting hurt.'

'Except David,' muttered Andrew as he withdrew his hands and placed them around his head, as if to push away all these troubling thoughts.

'Look at me my love,' beseeched Sandra, 'you can do this, we can do this, together. Then after he has gone, we shall be a couple, we can tell everyone and anyone.'

'I just don't know,' replied a troubled Andrew, 'it seems so wrong, I feel like I've betrayed my best friend. I have betrayed my best friend.'

'But he'd want us to be happy. He's always wanted you to have a loving long-term relationship, hasn't he?' nodded Sandra, seeking the same affirmative response from her lover. 'After all, he told me not to be lonely, he wanted me to meet someone else, someone kind and gentle, someone who would love and look after me. And I have. You. Just a bit earlier than planned. Who knows how long after bereavement is a decent enough time to fall in love again? This doesn't feel wrong to me; it feels ever so right. Just help me make his last few days comfortable and happy. Then we can be together without any guilt.'

'I really do hope so,' replied an unconvinced Andrew, 'I really do hope so, with all my heart.'

They were still sat next to each other in the relatives' room, each lost in their own thoughts, when a nurse knocked lightly on the door and walked in.

'We've made him more comfortable and have had to up the level of his painkillers to help ease his pain. His breathing is getting more laboured, I'm afraid he's nearing the end. I'm so sorry but hearing his stories over the last few weeks of his times with you both, well, he's had a good life. Not many can say that. He spoke lovingly about you both and he is so lucky to have you both here at the end.'

Sandra and Andrew looked at each other, both feeling guilt in their own way, for many different reasons. Andrew broke the silence, 'I've never seen anyone die nurse, what should I do.'

'Whatever feels right Andrew, perhaps hold his hand, both of you. What could be nicer than feeling the loving presence of both his long-term partner,' she smiled warmly at Sandra before turning back to Andrew, 'and his childhood friend. Tell him that you love him and will be with him again one day. Some family and friends even give permission for their loved ones to let go of life, to move on. Some dying patients feel they need that permission to leave their loved ones, others may pass on when the relatives leave the room, as if saving them the pain of seeing them draw their last breath. It is your journey with David, you have to do what you feel is right and follow his wishes.'

Andrew looked startled at this last comment. Did she know about them or had David confided about his fear of being buried and had he told the nurse, perhaps in the small hours when the human spirit is at its lowest, had he sought affirmation from her that it wasn't daft that he wanted his friend to be there at the undertakers when his coffin lid was finally screwed into place and to be there after the committal, to ensure he was cremated and not put into another deep and dark hole, one that he could not escape from.

'We are here love, Andrew and I,' said Sandra as she watched the slow rise and fall of David's chest. Each time it inflated and deflated she hoped that it would be the last, but inevitably it rose again. Through the gentle hiss of the oxygen she could hear the despairing prolonged sound of his struggling breath that seemed to rattle and wheeze, it pained her to see her other lover struggle so. Though his eyes were closed, as if in defiance of his pain, he reached out for his mask and lowered it to his chin, 'I have updated my will love, the solicitor came to see me a few days ago. I've made sure you

40

get what you deserve after all these years of loving me. I'm sorry I didn't marry you or couldn't have children,' he rasped out, words said with many struggled breaths between.

Sandra instinctively held her stomach that had life in it and looked anxiously at Andrew, who in turn looked shocked at her maternal reaction.

'No. Not that,' he thought. "They'd been so careful, though there was that one time in the car when they couldn't wait long enough to get home, their grief had reached out for comfort in the most basic and urgent of ways.' He smiled briefly at the memory of the illicit sexual encounter before realising how inappropriate it was. He was glad this smile went unnoticed.

Mistaking his shock for worry that David knew about their affair she gently shook her head as if to say, 'he couldn't possibly know, he's been either in hospital or this hospice.'

'You be at peace David,' she said reassuringly whilst holding his free hand, it felt so cold. 'You've been a wonderful partner. I have felt loved and cherished by you. Don't you worry about me, I'll be fine, but I will miss you, I love you.'

David took his other hand from the oxygen mask, as if to say that he was done with it, that he was ready to go. It slid down his chin and came to rest on his collarbone. With a great effort, he raised his other hand feebly, feeling and reaching out to his best friend. 'Remember your promise,' he weakly said as Andrew took his hand as it dropped onto the bed as his friend took his last breath. There was no need for Sandra to monitor the struggling rise and fall of his chest anymore. The trio were together for one last night.

'Thank you both for coming to see me,' said the solicitor as she guided Sandra and Andrew into her office with the open palm of her free hand. The other contained a small folder. 'Please sit down. I'm so sorry for your loss. I know that David has only just passed away and it is usual to have the last will and testament read out after the funeral, but David left some particular instructions.' She looked across to Andrew. 'He told me that he asked you to make a promise...'

'That's right,' interrupted Andrew, 'but I've no idea how I'll do it.'

'Yes, it is a rather unusual set of requests. It is normally a close loved one who asks to be present at the closing of the coffin. Another chance to say a final goodbye, though in this case he wanted you to make sure he was placed in the right coffin and with the correct nameplate.'

'That's right Ma'am, he was worried about being buried alive. He wanted no mistakes,' confirmed Andrew.

'Ah, I see, oh and please call me Jennifer,' she replied smiling at Andrew. She looked down at the will, though knew its contents by heart, such was the oddity of the request. 'David also requested that you be present at the cremation, that you are to make sure that he and his coffin are definitely cremated. I've never read out such a request and you can see now why I had to arrange for you both to come in days before the funeral. It's a specific and strange request though.'

'I'm afraid David developed a fear of dark enclosed spaces after we were trapped during a potholing expedition. That's why he took to rock climbing instead, he preferred the open spaces. As his cancer grew, he became fixated by being cremated.'

'Yes,' replied Jennifer now looking at Sandra, 'he was certainly troubled when I last saw him.'

'What about me,' interjected Sandra a bit too eagerly. 'I have the house and his savings, don't I?'

'Ah,' hesitated Jennifer, pulling off her reading glasses.

'What do you mean by ah?' questioned a suddenly frightful Sandra. 'I've been with him for five years, surely that entitles me to stay in the house and live off his savings?' she put her hand protectively to her stomach maternally again.

'I'm afraid that, as was his right, David changed his will in his last days from the one that you saw him make when you both last saw me here. He was still mentally aware, though his body was failing him.'

'But he still left me everything, his last will left me everything and I was to give Andrew any sports equipment he wanted. David knew I wasn't sporty.'

'I'm really sorry Sandra, but whilst he was still in sound mind, David left everything to Andrew.'

Sandra looked aghast, lost for words. Andrew looked equally shocked, 'but why would he do that?'

Jennifer looked across to them both, as if sizing them up and getting the measure of them. 'I'm afraid he did not specifically tell me, but he did keep saying that you both would get what you deserved.'

Sandra and Andrew were sat across from each other in a nearby café, nursing a steaming cup of coffee in their hands. 'Don't worry darling,' said Andrew between sips, 'I won't see you wronged. I'll get the house put into your name and give over his savings. He had quite a bit, hadn't he?'

Sandra was reluctant to tell him just how vast careful David's savings had been, ISAs, Premium Bonds, stocks, and shares; his portfolio had been increased greatly over the years. She was worried about Andrew becoming greedy, after all, bereaved families did strange things over money. David had earned such a lot over the years, so much so that he had been mortgage-free years ago and had planned well ahead for his early retirement. Would now be a good time to tell Andrew that she was pregnant with his child, or would this sudden announcement make her seem like a gold-digger, she pondered. She also suspected that poor David had discovered her secret on his deathbed.

'Err, yes, a fair old bit, saved over the years,' replied a hesitant Sandra. She caught the gleam in David's eye. Quickly changing the subject, she asked, 'how are you going to keep your promise to him, is that why he left you everything?'

'Do you think? It's an awful lot just to make sure he's correctly cremated. Do you think he suspected you were having an affair?'

'No, we were ever so careful, how could he possibly know about us?' she asked.

'I didn't mean with me, were you with other men, seeking your comfort whilst poor David was dying?'

'HOW DARE YOU!' she screamed as she stood up, her small stomach bump upending the table as she rose to leave. Coffee spilled onto Andrew's crotch burning through his trousers. In her anger, she'd forgotten about her extra bundle. 'I'm going home.' She stooped to pick up her handbag and felt the grip of Andrew's wet hand on her wrist.

'But it's not your home, is it, it's mine!'

Andrew tightened his black tie and looked across to the pews on the other side of the chapel. Sandra had not spoken to him in the last few days, other than to inform him of the funeral arrangements. He had tried to invite her to the chapel of rest, for the final time, at the local undertakers, but she had said she'd already been and had hung up the phone. He had wanted her there, not just because he still loved her and wanted to apologise for his inexcusable behaviour, but also because he was afraid. He had never been to an undertaker before, nor seen a dead body, other than when he had said a tearful goodbye to David at the hospice. He had needed the emotional strength from his lover. When he bent to kiss David's forehead at the hospice, soon after he had passed away, he had been surprised that he was still warm. This was his first emotionally painful experience of a dead body, and he had cried for his loss, and guilt, several times a day since.

45

Instead he went fearfully alone to the local undertakers. It hadn't been as bad as he had thought. The building was darkened with dim lights and his expectations of a dour morose elderly man were met. He even had the stooped slow gait that he had thought was typical of undertakers. But he was pleasantly surprised at how fearless he became once in the building. The doors to the other rest rooms were closed and he was taken into a brighter room, pleasantly decorated with pastel colours and a mural of two white doves flying gently between a floating cloud. In the far corner was a beautiful display of fresh flowers in a tall vase on a raised white ceramic plinth. He had also anticipated a rank smell, but there was none, even when he approached the open coffin to view his dead friend.

The dour undertaker had dressed David in his best suit and his old Corps tie from his army days. The same Corps that Andrew had joined so that they could stay together for those three years of service. David looked at peace, though you could easily gauge his weight loss from how the suit and shirt hung loosely on his withered frame. Andrew had bent over and stroked his hair and could finally say to David, 'I'm sorry mate, we simply fell in love, please forgive me. I will, somehow, honour your promise.' He then sat for about twenty minutes reminiscing about their good times, sometimes silently and sometimes spoken aloud as if talking to David. He even thanked him for generously leaving everything to him in his will.

And now, sitting in the crematorium chapel, watching it fill with people from David's life, he was furiously trying to work out how to get to the cremator room without being detected. He looked

46

reluctantly away from Sandra and to the door to the right of the curtains. He had worked out that the curtained area was where David's coffin would be taken to, away from the mourners, at the end of the service. 'So, the door must lead through there,' he thought.

During his walk around the building he had gauged the rough layout of the building. From the huge metal chimneys, that were already gently emitting soft clouds of white and grey smoke, he knew that the smaller, less ornate building was where the burning took place. Though he'd seen some sights in the army that would make a lesser man vomit or faint, he had worried that he wouldn't be able to go through with this. But a promise, is a promise, he had silently rebuked himself. Like a good soldier he had done his recce, on the internet, on YouTube, where he had watched several video clips of cremations in the UK. The coffin was never opened and was just slid into a furnace like container and simply burnt. Before the flames took hold, a heavy metal safety door was immediately closed over, thus preventing any viewing. Simple. He just had to slip through that door and watch undetected.

On the pretence of wanting to be the last to see the face of his dear friend, Andrew had gone to the undertakers earlier that morning and had witnessed the six ornate plume screws being put into place. Though they looked brass or gold, he was surprised to be told they were in fact plastic. Which made sense since it reduced the metalwork in the crematoria and lessened the risk of injury to the workers from explosions. The small amount of screws and nails in the coffin would cause no harm and would be easily removed amongst the ashes using

47

a strong magnet. The shiny brass nameplate, which Andrew had carefully read to ensure it had David's name and date of death and age, would burn as it was made of soft metal and the temperature would reach over one thousand degrees Celsius.

The speakers in the chapel crackled into life like someone stepping onto fallen autumnal leaves on a dry winter day. Hymnal music was gently played as mourners took the opportunity to clear their throats and give final coughs before their singing. The local vicar took to the lectern where below, the eagle held its wings proudly outstretched to envelope the bible from which she would read. She looked around the packed hall, briefly smiled that all-knowing, reassuring smile that is so familiar of all clergy, and began, 'We are here to remember and pay respect to our dear friend David who…'

Andrew tried to look like he was listening, but all the time he was thinking of that door, on how he could get through it unseen and seeing the others stand to sing, he stood up and a lightbulb moment went off in his head. He gave the briefest of smiles as he sang, 'Dear Lord and Father of Mankind, forgive our foolish ways…'

'We have but a short time to live,' said the vicar who reached down and pressed a button as she continued the committal words. Andrew watched sadly as heavy red curtains gently glided across his friend's coffin engulfing them within their fabric until he could no longer see the plinth on which he had silently reposed during the service, floral tributes resting gently above him, as if they were a quilt to warm his soul. Tears flowed from his eyes and ran down his cheek like a rivulet of rainwater from a heavy rainfall. His shoulders heaved

48

as he sobbed, alone, into the palms of his hands, as if shamefully hiding this open emotion. He sat hunched forward as he heard his fellow-mourners get to their feet and say together 'Amen' as the vicar had concluded with 'both now and ever.'

Andrew remained seated as a cascade of shuffling feet made their way out to view the wreaths that would have already been taken from atop David's coffin and had been placed in the Garden of Remembrance. He felt several firm hands placed on his shoulders as those who knew of his close friendship with David wanted to reach out and console this grieving friend. The last made him shudder as he felt a double tap as if a role reversal from David's time in the Hospice was returned. This last human touch made him look up through his tears to see the kindly vicar smiling down at him.

'You loved him very much didn't you?' she said as she sat down.

Andrew quickly looked around, surprised and relieved to see that they were alone, he had wept openly for several minutes whilst the chapel emptied, and the vicar had returned after numerous handshakes and muttered words of thanks from mourners.

'Yes. I did, Reverend, very much. I shall miss him. He was the best mate I ever had.' Something in him wanted to confess his guilt, though he was not a church goer, he felt he could unburden himself to her. 'I just feel so guilty.'

'That's a typical reaction to grief my friend, but please try not to dwell on it, David would not want you to feel guilt at his passing. I have heard from many what a good friend you were. Please take comfort from that. I'm afraid I must go now, as I have another funeral at my church and the traffic will be heavy at this time of day. But please feel free to call me or come to my church if you need some spiritual help.' She handed him a card with a photo of her church which had her e-mail address and telephone number on the back.

'Thank you, Reverend, I'll just sit here quietly and say a prayer for my friend if I may?'

'Of course, young man, you take as long as you need, this room isn't needed for another hour.' She gave him a double tap of his right hand, almost like she knew what he needed to confess through that familiar action.

Andrew smiled in appreciation and then bowed his head, as if in silent prayer. He heard her walk across the wooden floor and the swish and swoosh of a door open and close. He sat up with a grin on his face, and looked around at the empty chapel room, the first part of his plan had worked. Wasting no time, he quickly got to his feet and was soon at the door. Taking a deep breath to steady himself for the unknown sights of a crematoria room he pushed against the door whilst trying the doorknob, only to find it was locked. No amount of pushing would budge it. 'Damn!' he said aloud, before realising where he was and looking sheepishly around. He was relieved to see that he was still alone. Undeterred he initiated his Plan B, though he knew that this was more distasteful. He walked across to the heavy red curtains, took two deep breaths, and plunged himself behind them.

The wooden plinth, draped with a velvet cloth upon which was an ornately embroidered cross, was empty of David's coffin. He knew he had to be quick as his friend was already on his way to the furnace. With a distasteful look on his face he mounted the metal rollers that had been hidden by other curtains from the congregation and had efficiently carried his friend's coffin to the waiting trolley. Sitting upright, Andrew made his way along them, like a grocery item on a supermarket conveyer belt. He hoped that it would be a long time before he had need of this conveyance of the dead.

He entered a small room that held empty and open metal containers and a long-handled tool that resembled a rake that had lost its teeth. A few pegs on the walls held an assortment of what looked like aprons, gas masks and visor shields. Looking to the floor he saw the remnants of black rubber that displayed the route that the trollies had faithfully taken over the years and had ingrained their familiar track. He followed it and slowly and quietly opened the door.

An overweight, balding man, wearing an apron and blue disposable gloves was unscrewing the first of the six ornate plume screws from what he assumed to be David's coffin. Andrew silently slipped out his mobile phone, selected camera mode and recorded as the crematorium assistant placed each screw carefully in his pocket. As the sixth screw disappeared swiftly into his pocket Andrew stepped forward from the shadows of the door and asked, 'Is that to sell back to the undertaker? I thought such practices stopped in the 70's?'

'Jesus!' startled the wide-eyed ashen-faced assistant, 'what are you doing here. You gave me such a fright. How did you get in, I locked the door myself?'

Andrew smiled, now he knew that he could keep his promise. This man's greed had seen to that. He pointed to the curtains, 'the same way as my friend!'

'Well you can't be here; you've not had permission.'

'Permission?' queried a puzzled Andrew.

'The Superintendent didn't say that you'd be here. You did seek permission to watch the cremation, didn't you?'

'You mean that I could have legally watched my friend enter that?' asked Andrew pointing at the huge metal door that hung a metre or two above the floor.

'Why yes, two family members or close friends are permitted to see their loved one into the crematoria, didn't you know?'

'No, I didn't, otherwise I wouldn't have gone through your roller system,' he absently stroked his bruised bottom. 'My solicitor did wonder how I was going to do this, she never said that I could legally attend.'

'Pfft, what do solicitors know, they just take your money and make a few phone calls or write a few letters and charge you a fortune.'

'More to the point, why are you unscrewing my friend's coffin. That's not normal, is it?'

'Who cares, you are trespassing, now get out,' demanded the now composed assistant.

'No bother,' said Andrew casually waving his mobile phone, 'I'll just show this video to your Superintendent.' Noting another door, he pointed nonchalantly and said, 'through there, is it?'

'Wait a minute, don't be too hasty,' replied the overweight man, sweat beads starting to show on his forehead. 'What do you want?'

'I'll let you keep those screws, my friend won't mind too much, and you can keep your scam going, it looks to me like you need the extra money to buy those pies you are so fond of.' Andrew looked down at the man's paunch as if to emphasise his words and to try and intimidate him into giving him what he wanted. 'All I ask is that I watch my friend get cremated. You see I made him a promise and I want to keep it. He was afraid to be buried alive and wanted to make sure that I witness his cremation.'

The assistant looked oddly at him, shrugged, and then looked around the room. 'A bit weird, but okay, the Superintendent has already come through with the forms and verified your friend's identity from the nameplate. He won't be back until the next funeral in about an hour. That service will take another twenty minutes. But I do have to warn you, depending on your friend's weight it could take up to ninety minutes.'

'Don't worry about that,' replied Andrew sadly, 'the cancer ate him down to the bone, he won't take long to burn.' He shook his phone gently at the man, 'see that we are undisturbed, and I promise you that I'll delete this video. And remember that I always keep my promises.'

'Alright, let me just press a few buttons and push the coffin in, then the automatic machine does the rest. I'll get busy in the other room, out of the way of the Superintendent.'

As the assistant made to push the trolley holding David's coffin, Andrew called out quickly, 'wait a minute, let me just check the name plate. I want to do this right.'

He stepped up to the coffin and patted it twice, 'so long mate,' he said as he read the name plate. 'That's him alright.'

The assistant walked over and pushed the green button to the side of the crematoria. Andrew heard a sudden whooshing sound, as if a flame in an old-fashioned gas cooker had been lit. He could hear fans whirring from behind the machinery. Then the assistant walked back to the trolley.

'So how much do you get from the undertaker for those screws then?' asked Andrew.

The assistant's face went red, as if someone were strangling the life out of him, which is what Andrew would have liked to have done to him for stealing from his friend. 'Fifty pence each,' replied the embarrassed assistant.

'Is that all, you greedy miser! But then I guess you have several coffins a day, don't you? A nice little earner for you, isn't it? Your pockets must be bulging like your belly by the end of the day.'

The assistant took a step back, sensing the growing rage from this stranger.

'Okay, let's get on with it, shall we?' demanded Andrew, appalled at this man's greed. He watched fascinated as the crematoria door opened to reveal fireproof brickwork like a blacksmith's furnace. Blue flames spurted up from metal rimmed holes on the space where his friend would make his last earthly journey. As he turned back to the assistant, he was surprised to see that he had swiftly donned heavy-duty gloves and pulled on a facemask with glass visor.

'You'll need to take a few steps back mate, I don't want to explain why you got burnt.' He didn't say that he'd thought of overpowering this muscular man and putting him in with his friend. Though he knew he'd never be able to struggle with this fitter person, nor heave him onto the trolley. Besides, even this modern crematorium, designed for a fatter nation, would not hold two bodies. Though it did take mothers or fathers and their child if they died at the same time and the family wanted them to stay together. Even he had a conscience and would not steal from their combined coffin.

Andrew did as he was bid and watched as the trolley was expertly wheeled into the crematoria. It was quickly absorbed in dancing orange flames as the coffin ignited and burned. The assistant quickly closed the metal door. 'I'll be back to check the progress, please keep out of the Superintendent's way if you hear him come. I can't afford to lose my job.'

'No', thought Andrew wryly, 'you've a lucrative side-line going'. He nodded his acknowledgement, though he couldn't care less if this overweight buffoon lost his job. It would be better if a more caring person had the role. He didn't want to get himself in trouble and nodded again his agreement. He doubted he'd hear anyone approach anyway, above the sounds of the flames, the splintering of the coffin and bones and the heavy thrum of the extractor fans. He tried not to think of his friend's flesh crisping up and what little body fat he had fuelling the flames.

The assistant walked away and disappeared through the other door, leaving Andrew alone to hold his lonely, macabre vigil.

Andrew sat on the trolley, his bottom not afforded much comfort after the earlier encounter with the rollers. To take his mind from the crackling noises of his friend burning in the adjacent furnace and the whirring of the fans he took out his mobile phone and started flicking through various screens of his mobile. His attention was focused on the latest Facebook post of ScottishRecipes.co.uk, a site he'd recently visited to learn more about his grandfather's heritage, when he heard a double banging noise coming from the crematoria. He looked up and thought nothing of it, 'probably the wood of the coffin spitting out a knot,' he thought. He didn't like to think that the noise may have been bone finally being set alight as the skin, fat, muscle, veins, arteries, and organs of his friend had finally burnt through. He shuddered as he poignantly imagined his friend's heart aflame.

BANG, BANG, repeated the noise. Andrew looked up startled. Two bangs, like the double tap of his friend's hand, 'surely not!' he thought as he tentatively wiggled down from the trolley whilst pocketing his phone, all thought of his discomfort gone.

BANG, BANG, continued the noise which Andrew knew was coming from inside the furnace. He wished that the fat assistant was here to allay his primal fears, despite his repugnancy to the man.

BANG, BANG, insisted the noise, much louder now. Andrew stood rigidly to attention, as if he were a meerkat alerted to danger.

Inside he was shaken to the core. 'Was this normal?' he thought to himself.

BANG, BANG, went the eerily familiar rhythmic noises which now sounded like cannonballs released at the beginning of an ancient battle. Andrew couldn't help himself; it was as if he were hypnotised or in a deep, but vivid dream where reality was slowly playing out. He found himself walking the few feet to the furnace door. As if sensing his wary footsteps, the noises ceased, his attention had been grasped and held, he was summoned and was on his way.

Andrew found himself at the furnace door, he could feel the heat emanating from the crematoria, the contrast in temperature was like walking from a comfortably air-conditioned aircraft into the heat, haze, and humidity of a foreign runway. Only he somehow knew that what was going to happen to him would be no holiday.

BANG, BANG, double thumped the noise as if in agreement. 'Welcome to a nightmare,' it seemed to say unspoken into Andrew's mind. He remained riveted to the spot again, unable to move, though fearful of what he might now experience.

As if reading his thoughts, the crematoria door burst open and omitted a whoosh of fierce heat that spread throughout Andrew's body. His breath was taken from deep within his lungs as the air exchange took place. Panic filled his mind as he found himself fighting for life-saving breath. Curiously though, he could still rationally look down at his hands and body. They remained the same, not burnt as he would have expected, just the soul-sucking struggle for air.

His eyes were drawn to what remained of his friend and his coffin. He jealously looked on as air from the back fan whizzed around the dark ash and the blackened bony fragments that remained of his friend on the large metal tray. It was almost as if in the powdery residue he could briefly make out the outline of the emaciated frame of David.

Andrew stooped over suddenly, the need to breathe becoming more frantic. Despite this basic yearning for survival he still could not take his eyes from the ash and bone residue. His eyes widened as they were whipped up in a tempestuous frenzy, like a tornado hitting a dull sandy beach. The blackened greyish ash rose as one and formed a circle, the dull powder started to glow as if breath was given to the earthly residue to reignite the dying embers. Andrew looked on in disbelief as the face of his long dead friend was shaped before him. A hand, aflame and burning fiercely formed in front of this phantom face and with palm outstretched it reached up to the ember aglow lips. They pursed and blew out lifesaving, but cancerous ridden air which danced around the furnace before making its journey deep into the lungs of the still stooped Andrew. His face remained raised in this strange pose that resembled an old man gasping for air whilst desperately looking around him for help.

As he sucked in the cancerous and ember glowing particles that accompanied the ghostly breath, Andrew heard himself wheeze in deeply with an ominous groaning sound that sounded like the distant tolling of a death knell. His eyes remained rigidly focused inside the furnace where the glowing particles were still playing out their macabre dance to the movement of the rear fans. They darted and weaved like little pixies cavorting to the music of a forest nymph as they shaped and formed themselves back into the face of David. The spectre winked at Andrew, formed his open palm into a single finger that waggled from side to side like a father telling an errant son off, before breaking up and disappearing into the hollow cavity of this grisly form's mouth, from which a deep, rasping chuckle emitted and twirled and jigged around his former friend's mind, destined to repeat itself ghoulishly for the last few months of Andrew's pain ridden life…

Author's Note

Aye, a bittie strange! Don't ask me where this short story came from, you are not permitted into the macabre workings of my dark mind! Only I can cope with the monsters that beat the door and visit me in the wee small hours as I narrowly escape Mrs Buswell carting me off to a special place of safety and treatment!

But if you see me looking absently away with a small smile on my face, just know that the inner mechanisms of my brain are saying, 'what if...'

Do let me know what you thought of this small, sinister outing, perhaps with a review at Amazon.co.uk or GoodReads.com and even on my Facebook page at facebook.com/cgbuswell and twitter.com/CGBUSWELL

Can you see that shadow, just behind your left shoulder? His evil malevolent desire grows stronger each day...

Thanks

Chris

Acknowledgements

There's another stunning piece of art adorning the front cover by my lovely daughter Abigail. As this is a compendium, you'll have to visit my website to see it. Perhaps it is best that you've never read any of my works Abigail, or you'd be thinking of my nursing home decades before you need too! If, dear reader, you need a Hons Degree in Painting artist then visit her site at abibuswell.wordpress.com

Thank you, 'Padre' Katherine and Ray Hyman of Cruden Bay IT Services, www.crudenbaytraining.co.uk for the proof-reading and spotting the howling mistakes with your red pens and for going along with the stories and advising me on how to improve my craft.

The lettering for the cover and maintenance of my author website at www.cgbuswell.com is from the talented Richard at www.rogue.co.uk who is so much better with colours and fonts than me and who always produces such creative work. Thank you, Richard.

Thank you to Heather at Coffin Works in Birmingham for such a fascinating tour and talk about coffin furniture. Visit this interesting museum at www.coffinworks.org

Christmas at Erskine

By C.G.Buswell

Scott closed the door to the Personnel Recovery Centre in Edinburgh, grateful for the accommodation just a short drive from Combat Stress where he had been undergoing therapy. As he made his way to his car, he enjoyed the feel of the crunch of his shoes on the virginal snow as it crackled down and sunk slightly, relishing the experience of each footstep, feeling a little taller with each stride. He still had a long way to go before accepting and conquering his condition of Post-Traumatic Stress Disorder, and much more therapy to overcome his anxiety, beating headaches and low morale. As he enjoyed looking up at the nearby trees and listening to the birds twitter their morning song he thought grimly back to his encounter with the Grey Lady and Naomi. He dared not tell his therapists and support worker about that ordeal, nor did he confide in Padre Caldwell, though he did enjoy his visits and the boxes of chocolates. Instead he had told them about how anxious he had become; how he had locked himself away in his flat and had taken too much codeine for the headaches which beat away, almost like someone pounding directly onto his temple with a heavy stick and penetrating deep into his psyche, changing his character. Scott concentrated on enjoying the freshness of the Scottish air and looked up to see the sun glaring out around him. It was teasing him and the others getting out of their cars in the adjacent car park. Lovely and bright but deceptive for it was cold and he shivered, not just because of the low temperature but because of his remembering the encounters with the ghost and her legacy that she said left him with special insight. Had he been haunted or caught up in a freak fantasy to escape the horrible truth? He only wished he could have the ability to cure himself of negative thoughts, feeling guilty about surviving Afghanistan when others did not. But he must move on and put these hallucinations behind him and think more positively. He opened his car boot and lifted in his kitbag and quietly closed the boot: he still could not tolerate loud noises.

Over in the adjacent car park, mere metres away, were three elderly ladies, smartly dressed in slacks and thick woollen coats. Each wore a shiny scarlet and silver badge that glinted in the winter sun and caught Scott's eye. He smiled. He recognised the badges as large sized emblems of the QA Association with its large crown above the cross of the Order of Dannebrog chosen by Queen Alexandra to represent her native Denmark. She also chose the motto Sub Cruce Candida as the motto for her beloved QAs which meant under the white cross. The Association rather than having the motto on their emblem chose Friendship instead. Scott knew he needed more friends to help him after his bereavement and these were former members of the Queen Alexandra's Royal Army Nursing Corps, his fellow nurses, long retired, but still active within the Association. Scott had been ordered, by Colonel Kirsty Duncan, his matron of 22 Field Hospital, to attend the coffee morning at the opposite building, Erskine Nursing Home. This was one order he gladly accepted; indeed, it wasn't as much an order as a suggestion.

'You'll love it Scott, you're a war hero, three tours of active conflict, a chest full of medals and a recent deployment to Sierra Leone, they'll be all over you with their cakes and coffee, just don't have breakfast! If you don't eat a slice of each lovingly baked cake,

65

you'll offend at least one former QA and I don't want to hear from an old matron or ward sister that you refused their shortbread!' she laughingly told him. 'Besides, you need fattening up. Take plenty of change so that you can buy raffle tickets and if you win wine bring it back for me! Oh, and take something for their bring and buy sale, books usually sell well, and make sure you buy something.'

'But I've never been to a QA coffee morning before, can't I just drive straight home to Aberdeen for my Christmas leave Ma'am?' asked a hopeful Scott.

'Ha no way boyo,' she boomed, 'this is one duty I insist on. The QA Association isn't just for retired nurses and health care assistants or admin staff, it's also for serving members. Above all it is about friendship and helping those in their time of need and frankly Scott you need both. So, when you leave the PRC do a left turn and enjoy the coffee morning. It's at Erskine Care Home, just next door, which only accepts patients who have had military service or their spouses. I've heard good things about the care they receive and hope to see it for myself one day. In the meantime, when I visit you at Tidworth in February, I expect to hear all about it – and see that you are on the mend and eager to re-join us. In the meantime, please continue with your therapy sessions and enjoy being home in Scotland.' With that she had briskly turned and left.

Scott was grateful that she and the Second in Command had arranged for his rehab and PTSD treatments.

Scott walked carefully across the snow to follow the ladies into the nursing home and what a pleasant building it looked with its

66

modern curving architecture over two levels. He'd read that it had opened in 2002 with a further extension to cope with the demand in 2009. Yet from outside both buildings seamlessly fitted as if built in the same initial construction. Though it was the depths of winter the gardens had been immaculately weeded and were awaiting the colour that spring brings. The evergreen plants cheered the area up and seemed to be a haven for eager birds pecking away for worms and other grubs. As he entered the Reception area, he smiled at the sight of the tall Christmas tree which was adorned with plentiful decorations and tinsel. A white dove in flight carrying a festively wrapped Christmas box in its beak caught his eye and his grin broadened as he thought of his father and his beloved doos, the pigeons and doves that Naomi had so loved. How would his father feel about his breakdown and should he tell him? As he paused to read the brass sign that announced that HRH Princess Royal opened the building on the 14 November 2009 his thoughts were interrupted:

'Ah ma bonnie loon, you must be Scott?' enquired a cheerful woman dressed in matching skirt and jacket with a dark and light blue, scarlet and white silk scarf tied neatly over the top of her blouse. She was effortlessly carrying a wide box and was speaking his Doric dialect so Scott knew she must have travelled down from his Granite City for the occasion.

'Aye,' replied Scott hesitantly. 'I'm here for the QA coffee morning.'

'Well make yourself useful and carry in my cupcakes, but be gentle mind, I was up early this morning icing them. And watch you don't step on Figaro.' She cheerfully handed the white box over to Scott, 'I'm Fiona, Kirsty told me to expect you. I'm under orders to look after you. I thought my days of orders from Matrons were long over. Still, it makes me feel useful. The room is along this way. We're in the Robertson Trust Room, lovely and warm. We used to hold them in the Garrison Church, but one year we couldn't book their rooms and our Colonel found this place. A great find, isn't it special? Perhaps I should book a room.'

'Och no Ma'am you look lively and young enough,' replied Scott as he struggled to keep up with her quick pace, wondering who, or what Figaro was.

'Ha, ha, I was told you were charming to the ladies. None of the Ma'am stuff with me ma loon, I only reached the dizzy heights of Sergeant. In fact, we're all friendly here, all first names and no mention of rank, you'll have fun.'

Scott didn't look too convinced but obediently followed and couldn't help but grin at the sign that said to watch out for Figaro the dog wandering around. He felt he was being led much like a faithful animal. As he entered the room he gave it a quick scan and saw other ladies busy at tables, unpacking an assortment of tasty looking cakes, piles of DVDs and books and handmade crafts such as a fun looking reindeer face made from card which had a red lollipop inserted to look like a nose. He must get one for his dad he cheekily thought.

'Hello Scott, I'm Morag the branch secretary, it's a pleasure to meet you. I've heard so much about you,' lowering her voice she added, 'what you and our boys and girls did in Sierra Leone was incredible, we're all proud of you.' Sensing Scott's embarrassment she quickly added, 'Maybe one day you'll tell us all about it, in the meantime would you like a cup of tea or coffee?' Picking up a saucer and cup she quickly added a millionaire shortbread, 'I baked these myself, I'd love to ken what you think of them,' she enquired.

'They look delicious, lovely and thick chocolate, just how I like them, coffee please Morag.'

Morag beamed at his compliment as she poured out his coffee and handed him the saucer and cup, 'milk and sugar are on the side there, then come and join us girls for a gossip,' she nodded to the table by the bring and buy stall which had several empty chairs scattered around a small group. 'But don't feed any to Figaro, apparently he's had his ration of cake this week from the ladies at Erskine.'

Scott bit into his millionaire's shortbread. As he chewed, he enjoyed the crunch of the set chocolate and then the mingling of the toffee that formed a sweetly gooey mess that stuck to his teeth. He munched down onto the shortbread and marvelled at this excellent Scottish recipe that combined several of his favourite ingredients to form one of his favourite treats. 'Mmm, affa tasty Morag, I ken a Padre who would love these,' said Scott as he beamed at her.

Morag blushed but this was hidden as Fiona, not to be outdone, stretched across with a plate of cranberry flapjacks and buttered drop scones, 'Do try these dear, just like granny made!'

'They sure do look nice, thank you,' replied Scott, helping himself to one of each, grateful for being pre-warned by the Colonel not to have breakfast. He discretely counted the ladies around the room and worked out that he had at least sixteen more cakes and biscuits to munch through. He quickly tried to work out unique compliments to say for each one. He also noted that he wasn't the only male; there was an elderly gentleman, dressed in tartan trousers and smart light green jacket with a silk tie with striped colours of green, gold, navy and black. He was sat by a chair at the other door petting a young red dachshund.

'Do you remember Major Maugham from BMH Iserlohn?' asked Fiona to Morag.

'Do I!' laughed Morag. 'She was a right ogre, gave me restrictions of privileges for three nights in a row because my frilly hat wasn't starchy enough. She said it was as floppy as a wet dishcloth. She ran that medical ward like she was a Sergeant Major.'

'Well I met her at the Cenotaph last week, and she still thinks she's an RSM! Had us all lined up and practicing our marching before the parade. Mind you it paid off; we were all in step.' She was interrupted by several barks from Figaro, who was jumping up between barks. 'What's he up to now, jumping up for no reason, daft dog! But isn't it lovely to see such a bonnie dog in a care home, I bet he'll make a wonderful therapy dog when he's finished being a playful puppy. He belongs to Jenny, charming girl, she works here in the recreation department.' Morag gave a little laugh, 'He keeps pinching the bowls when the residents play boccia bowls! They usually find it amusing, but not when they were practicing for the recent Erskine

Commonwealth Games. All four care homes in Scotland took part, great fun.'

Scott looked across to the dog as the conversation moved on to talk about the friends both women had in common. He now recognised her from the BBC coverage of the Cenotaph parade that he had watched at the PRC on his ipad. He had so wanted to go to church to pay his respects, but his anxiety had proved too much. He had felt so guilty at what he thought had been disrespect but had stood for the minute silence and had proudly watched the Festival of Remembrance the night before. He was so proud to have seen his colleague from Sierra Leone and shed many tears as she talked about her ordeal of developing Ebola and how she thought she may die. They had all secretly thought that. It had brought back painful memories for Scott. But he had been so proud of her delivering the Book of Remembrance across the Albert Hall. Like her, he knew he would heal one day and get on with his army career. As he looked around him, he was grateful for the friendship of so many QAs. His eyes were drawn once more to the man playing with the dog. He looked too old to have served with the QAs, since men were only admitted to the Corps in 1992. Scott excused himself from the group and walked over to him. He bent down to stroke the dog and introduced himself to the man. 'Hello, I'm Scott, I recognise the colours on your tie, it's the Gordon Highlanders isn't it?'

'Aye laddie, I served many a year with the Gordons, and proudly so.'

'So, you're an Aberdeen loon then?' enquired Scott eagerly.

'Nae quite loon, up a bittie at Fraserburgh.'

'Aye I ken it fine, the Broch ma faither calls it.'

'Aye, after the auld Scots word for Burgh. So, fit brings you here the day?'

'My Matron asked me to come along and make new friends from the QA Association. But I'm guessing you've never been in the QAs yersel, are you a husband of one of the wifies here?' asked Scott switching easily back into his Doric dialect of Aberdeenshire.

'Naw lad, I often come along here to listen tae the quines blethering awa. I wanted to see this daftie here,' he bent down to pet Figaro once again. 'He's a bonnie loon is this laddie, I love dogs, such sensitive creatures. He's so gentle with us residents, but a bit of a feartie.' He chuckled as he continued, 'he'll catch his own reflection in the piano during singalongs and growl away.'

Scott extended his arm and proffered his hand, 'I'm Scott by the way.'

'Pleased to meet you Scott, I'm Jim.' said the man, taking Scott's hand in both of his. 'Please excuse my cold hands.'

'Nae bother, so what brought you to Erskine if you don't mind me asking, you look fine and healthy.'

'Aye richt enough, but I wisnae always. Fine bunch of nurses and carers here. Nothing is too much trouble. When I left my home to stay here, I didn't expect to have so much fun. Especially after my Peggy died. Oh, she was a lovely lass. Grief and loss are so hard to bear isn't it?'

'Aye, it is that,' replied Scott with a sigh. 'I recently lost someone who I loved deeply; it's so hard to move on.'

'It is that laddie, it is that. Sorry to hear that; and you so young tae.' At that moment Figaro barked and wagged his tail, nose pointing to the door. 'Here, let me show you around the home and you'll get the chance to watch Figaro run up and doon the corridor. Could you open the door for us please?'

Scott obliged them both and Figaro bolted for the opened door, made a sharp right turn by the kitchens and was off. Jim followed him and Scott went through the door, catching a glance at the group of QAs watching him with concerned looks. 'Maybe just a quick look round Jim, I'm supposed to be mooching around at the coffee morning.' Passing the kitchen Scott remarked, 'Lunch smells good.'

'Aye, you always eat well here.' Jim noticed Scott frowning at some old black and white framed photos on the walls of nurses with patients. Most looked fit and well, though there were some sat on old-fashioned wheelchairs and were missing legs. They all looked smart in the matching pyjamas and even the amputees had their trouser legs smartly pinned back. The nurses looked spotless in the white starched aprons and white veils. They reminded Scott of the Grey Lady and he again involuntary shivered, though the home was warm. 'You've had quite the ordeal recently haven't you Scott? An old veteran soldier can always tell, some call it the thousand-yard stare.'

Scott was momentarily taken aback, almost thinking that Jim knew about the Grey Lady. 'I know what you mean Jim. I've recently come back from Africa and before that Afghanistan. I saw some awful things, but also some great things, the miracle of modern medicine and nursing I guess.'

'Ah ha laddie, much like these chaps in the photo. They are patients of Craiglockhart Hospital which was here in Edinburgh. They cared for the psychologically damaged, what the War Office called neurasthenia. I guess you'd called it battle-shock or PTSD. The building is now used as part of the Napier University Campus. Here at Erskine we were asked to suggest names for the wards and Sassoon and Owen were so popular that they were chosen.'

'After the war poets?'

'That's richt son. More sensitive souls. They could convey the horrors of war in such beautiful poems.'

'I've read some by Robert Graves, wasn't he a patient too?'

'Nae lad,' corrected Jim, 'people often say that, but they are mistaken. He only visited his friend Siegfried Sassoon and in fact escorted him here to be admitted.'

'Oh.' Scott chastised himself. 'I should have kent that, military history is a hobby of mine.'

'Ah well you'll love these pictures further up the corridor then Scott,' said Jim leading the way past murals of flowering poppies in fields. 'These are of passing out parades of some of the Scottish regiments, including my old regiment The 1st Battalion The Gordon Highlanders.'

Scott walked further along the corridor whilst Figaro dashed up and down, his back legs barely able to keep up with the pace of his front legs. Scott chuckled away at his antics as he passed each watercolour. He was so impressed with the artists' detail, you could practically reach out and touch the lifelike scenery, almost expect the soldiers to start marching off. The next picture was a collage of many photographs and reading the caption above Scott could see they were of Royal family visits.

'Do you see Prince Charles in amongst them?' enquired Jim.

Scott looked more closely and spotted him, kilted, and wearing a Gordon Highlanders tie. He peered closer at the man Prince Charles was talking with and then Scott looked at Jim.

'Aye laddie, that's me. One of the proudest days of my life. He was our last Colonel-in-Chief. He chatted away with me like we were auld friends. Wonderful man, loved us Highlanders.'

'Fantastic,' said an impressed Scott, 'our Colonel-in-Chief is Her Royal Highness The Countess of Wessex. I'd love to meet her one day. She always wears a poppy with the QA badge engraved on it at Remembrance events.'

'Aye, a bonnie lassie, next door is my room, look Figaro is sitting outside it. May I show you?'

'Aye, please, but not if I'm intruding or taking up your time.'

'I've all the time in the world Scott, come on in. Could you get the door please and let Figaro in?'

Scott obliged and noted Jim had his full name on the door along with a lovely photograph of him smiling away, though he looked frailer in the image. He held the door open and Jim went in and popped himself onto his comfortable armchair.

Scott sat opposite him in the guest chair, just outside the en-suite bathroom. 'So, did you see much action in the Gordon's Jim?'

'Aye, too bloody much! I was in Tampin in Malaya, what you'd now call Malaysia. It was never officially a war. The Governments called it an Emergency, but it lasted from 1948 through to 1960 and was just as brutal as any other armed conflict. I went out as a young nineteen-year-old, green as anything, along with my best mate Ally. You could say that we went out as boys and left men. Or at least I did. We were fighting the Communist Terrorists and they were unforgiving. Hard fighters they were, and the sad thing is that they were trained by our troops during the Second World War so were taught to kill well. Being local they knew how to blend into the jungle and vanish. Such thick impenetrable jungle, it took us days to navigate through to our targets. Even when we were there in 1952 things were still basic. We fought for each other, but the politicians fought for the valuable rubber and palm oil and timber and tin. We didn't care for any of that, we just wanted to survive and go home. There had always been Chinese in Malaya and they fought for the British Colony in this revolt and insurgency. There was heavy loss on both sides and me and my mates took lives, not an easy thing to do, but a duty we had trained for. I envy you Scott, saving lives instead of taking them.' Jim looked out of the window, doing his own thousand yards stare with tears in his eyes.

'It sounds like Ally never made it home?' enquired Scott gently.

76

'I knew when I first saw you Scott that you had great empathy. You have great understanding. She was right you know.'

Scott looked surprised and a chill ran through his body as he incredulously thought of what Jim meant, surely not he thought.

Jim continued, ignoring Scott, but taking the time to reach down and stroke Figaro behind his ear. 'There was no emergency helicopters or highly qualified nurses and doctors for us unfortunately. The Medical Emergency Response Team was decades away from being. We were deep in the jungle with our Iban trackers, trying to root out CT's, the Communist Terrorists, to burn down their bases and kill or capture them. Only this time we were vastly outnumbered. We were commanded to perform a tactical retreat and during this Ally got shot in the stomach whilst defending our platoon's retreat. We all knew he was a goner. Even if we could have got a chopper below the thick jungle canopy he would not survive. And the worst thing was that Ally knew it. We didn't have much time, he asked for some grenades off the boys. I couldn't bring myself to give him mine; I knew what he had in mind. I didn't even know what to say to him. Certainly, none of this love you man or hugging that you youngsters do now. I could only bring myself to pat him on the shoulder and wish him luck. I knew what he was about to do when we got clear and the CTs were upon him.'

Scott listened in awe; his earlier confusion forgotten.

'You're a good listener Scott, no wonder you were chosen. You've quite a journey to go on and I wish you well. Yes, Ally took out the advancing CTs and bought us time to get away at the cost of his own life. And ever since I've never been able to forgive myself,' finished Jim as tears silently fell down his cheeks.

Scott understood now. He reached over to Jim's hands and as he took them, he said, 'Ally understood Jim. Just like every soldier understands. He bravely and willingly did his duty. He does not blame you, he's proud to have saved so many of his friends and fellow Highlanders. He's been at peace all these years. Don't ask me how I know this, I just do. It's a special gift I've recently developed and I'm only just getting used to having it. My own guilt and loss were getting in the way, but I'm on the road to recovery.'

'That's good to hear Scott, and thank you,' said Jim through his tears. He looked out of his window and removing his right hand from Scott's he pointed to a round patio area with freshly planted shrubs and a beautifully ornate sandstone bird table as a centre piece. I've always loved that view. The patio area was donated to Erskine from the Royal Horticultural Society Chelsea Flower Show, all the way from London. It's our contemplation garden, I shall miss it. Thank you, Scott. You ken his drumming is only going to get louder.'

Scott felt Jim's other hand slip from his own. When he looked away from the window to Jim's chair, he was not at all surprised to see it was now empty. He felt no fear, only a huge sense of peace as he turned to Jim's bed where he was laid out in his smart dark green with yellow stripe Gordon Highlanders kilt and jacket. His hands were clasped over his body where a thoughtful nurse had helped his cooling body to grasp once more his much-loved Glengarry immaculate with its red and white diced pattern. His brown Tam o

Shanter was proudly on display on his bedside cabinet with the Gordon's regimental cap badge with the motto By Dand jutting out from under the Stag's head from the tartan square background. The nurses and carers had done a touching job of making Jim look his best once more for his friends and family to see him before going to the undertakers. Scott noticed a wet line running down Jim's cheek, like a rogue tear from a long-held memory being released. He pulled out the handkerchief from his suit pocket, just above the QARANC blazer badge and dabbed Jim's cheek dry. 'Go in peace mate.'

After a moment of prayer and thought Scott looked down to Figaro who was sat squarely at the foot of Jim's bed and said, 'C'mon boy.' They both left the room quietly, Scott closing the door behind him. He walked back down the corridor, Figaro trotting happily by his side, tail gently wagging in rhythm to his movement. 'Clever boy Figaro, you dogs have the gift too, don't you?' As if in reply Figaro gave a small, but happy bark and ran to the Robertson Trust Room whose door was just opening.

'Ah, there you are Scott, we were beginning to wonder if us girls had frightened you off. Come along with us as we browse round the Erskine Christmas Fayre, you can help carry the goodies we buy.'

Scott obediently fell in line with his new friends. He knew that this Christmas and many more would not be as lonely as he thought.

*****

Scott's adventures continue in The Drummer Boy. Read the first chapter of my first novel The Grey Lady Ghost of the Cambridge

Military Hospital: Part 1 of the Grey and Scarlett series for free at www.cgbuswell.com where there are links to buy it in Paperback or on Kindle.

It would help this fledgling author's career if you would please leave a review at Amazon or Good Reads or tell your friends about it using the social media links below or on the right if you loved this story.

If you have enjoyed this Christmas short story, then please consider a donation to the veterans' charity Erskine who care for veterans and their spouses since 1916 at www.erskine.org.uk

To learn more about the QARANC Association please visit www.qarancassociation.org.uk and for the history of the Corps please visit www.qaranc.co.uk and if you need to look up the Doric words used then try the A-Z at www.doricphrases.com

Acknowledgments

A big thank you to Stewart Pebbles for showing me around Erskine and giving me so many nuggets of information. Thank you to Judith Haw, External Communications Officer at Erskine for kindly allowing me to use Erskine as a setting and for arranging a tour of their wonderful Home at Edinburgh. I'm grateful to Jenny of their Recreation Department for allowing me to share Figaro with readers.

I'd also like to say a BIG THANK YOU to readers as I embark on a full-time writing career and for your kind words of encouragement on Facebook, Twitter and through your reviews and for following and believing in Scott and his adventures.

I love that my gifted daughter, Abigail, and my wife, Karla, created the covers for this Christmas short story. Both are such talented artists. Abigail's is on Amazon whilst Karla's is on my website. Which do you prefer?

The lettering and website are from the talented Richard at www.rogue.co.uk who with a few words brief always produces such creative work.

I'm indebted to Padre Katherine and Ray Hyman of Cruden Bay IT Services www.crudenbaytraining.co.uk for their continuing support and proof reading. Merry Christmas guys and see you at the Kirk at midnight.

Halloween Treat

By C.G. Buswell

Scott calmed his inhalation and exhalation, conscious only of each steady rhythmic breath in and out. This was an important shot and he couldn't afford to miss. His target was in front of him and he was ready to unload, to hit his mark. He'd aimed and his hands were steady. He showed no nerves and concentrated as he aligned slightly to take in the environmental factors. His trigger finger was ready to plunge the payload. He focused on his heartbeat and could make out the steady 65 beats per minute that he knew his resting pulse to be. He committed himself to taking the shot on his next breath when his diaphragm and breathing muscles would be most relaxed. This was it he told himself, this is what all those years of training had been about. He slowly breathed in and felt the correct tightness and maintained his aim and committed himself as he held the fruit firm and plunged the toy syringe into the orange. 'And that's how you give an injection Thomas.'

'Cor Scott, let me try,' said an excited Thomas as he jumped up and down at the kitchen table, his youthful blonde hair bobbing up and down with each eager leap.

Scott laughed, 'Alright ma wee loon,' he said to the young lad who was used to the funny words and sayings that Scott came out with. His mum thought that Scott was calling him a loony when he first said it and Scott had to explain to her a few days later that it was Aberdonian Doric for young lad or boy and not an insult. So began a regular tutorial of the North East of Scotland dialect between the threesome. They were now quite used to Scott's peculiar dialect and phrases and now he was a trusted baby-sitter. This suited Wendy fine since she and Thomas lived in the flat next door to Scott.

On this occasion Wendy had popped out for an hour, for a meeting at work and had left Thomas showing Scott his new play nursing outfit of white tunic and trousers and most importantly of all, the toy medical equipment and bag. This was a favourite plaything of Thomas' as it had been given as a gift by Scott for his seventh birthday last month. He was now taking off the tiny stethoscope from around his neck and was reaching into his black medical bag with the white cross transfer in the centre, looking for another needleless toy syringe. As Scott had shown him, he took out the toy drug vial and pretended to draw up some fluid, checking for air bubbles and flicking them to the top to be pushed out by the plunger.

'That's right, isn't it Scott?'

Scott laughed again, 'aye my bonnie wee loon; you've the makings of a great nurse.'

'An army nurse like you Scott?'

'Aye, but maybe even better,' teased Scott.

Thomas looked with evident pride to the other side of the table, 'Will I get lots of medals like yours Scott?'

'I don't see why not ma wee mannie, if you work hard enough,' replied Scott as he too looked across to see his Iraq, Afghanistan, and other medals. His latest addition to the collection was awarded for nurses, medical and support staff that had nursed and cared for patients with Ebola in the Kerry Town treatment centre at Sierra Leone. He considered this to be the hardest earned medal of his career, even worse than what he went through in The Stan, seeing Naomi and her comrades killed. Operation Gritrock would stay with him for a long time because of the dying children. He looked fondly back to Thomas, touched that his mother honoured him with the trust of caring for him as a reliable baby-sitter despite knowing about his psychiatric troubles from his Post Traumatic Distress Order. He was grateful that the walls of this new housing development, Wellesley, named after the Duke of Wellington, so famed for the Battle of Waterloo, was lined with acoustic soundproofed plasterboard sheets that did not let his screams and cries of the night penetrate through to their bedrooms. God knows what they would have made of the noises when he was visited by, (or did he imagine?), the Grey Lady ghost that was said to have haunted this building, the site of the old Cambridge Military Hospital in Aldershot.

'That's the way Thomas, hold the orange firmly and remember if it were really skin you would pull it taut, slightly stretching it,' he coaxed gently.

Thomas, ever eager, plunged the syringe into the orange, causing it to push through the peel and pith. 'I did it Scott, look!'

'Aye, well done Thomas!' he said, not wanting to burst his bubble of excitement in telling him that a real patient would not like to be stabbed and have a syringe sticking out of their bottom like that. He also didn't bother advising Thomas to aspirate the plunger to see if any blood returned into the syringe; a sign that the needle had hit a blood vessel. If he ever became a real nurse using a real needle, then Scott hoped his nursing tutors would also teach him about avoiding needle stick injuries and the safe disposal of needle and syringe. His thoughts were interrupted by the sounds of Wendy entering the flat.

'Cooeee,' she shouted through the lobby. 'How's my favourite two nurses doing?' she joked. 'You haven't been listening to each other's heart-beats again have you?'

Thomas scooped up his orange, still with the lethal weapon sticking out and ran excitedly to his mother. 'Look what I've done mummy, I've given my first injection.'

'Well done you, Thomas. And did the patient survive?'

'Aye mum,' replied Thomas, using his favourite Scottish word, 'he is pain free now.'

'That's great news. I hope you've been behaving yourself for Scott?'

'Aye mum, he showed me his medals too.'

Wendy laughed, 'What? Again!'

'Aye, and he said that maybe one day I'll get as many as him when I'm an army nurse.'

'What! You're going to leave me all alone and travel the world?' kidded Wendy, pulling an unhappy face.

'I'll come back and visit though mummy, then I can show Scott my own medals,' said Thomas quickly, wanting to stop his mum looking unhappy.

'Ha,' joined in Scott, 'and I'll be an old mannie sitting in a rocking chair with a blanket, admiring your shiny medals and hearing your tales of adventures.' He stooped over and pretended to shuffle along to pick up his medals. 'Good meeting?' he inquired of Wendy as he finally straightened up.

'Yes, very productive, shame the management called it on my day off though. But we're to get a pay rise, so it was worth going along to. Thanks so much for looking after Thomas at such short notice.' She turned to her son, 'And I've got the last part of your Halloween costume in my bag.'

'Let me see, let me see,' demanded Thomas as he jumped up and down once more.

'Nope. Not until Scott's gone, I don't want to spoil the surprise for when you go trick or treating him.'

'Guising is what we call it up in Scotland ye ken,' said Scott.

'Eh,' said a puzzled Thomas and Wendy at the same time.

'It's the same as your trick or treating but the word came from the disguises the children wear. I guess over the years it evolved into the new word, guising. But our laddies and lassies still have to perform a short song, dance, or tell a joke. Some of the bairns even recite a poem, though I prefer the song "Ye cannae push yer grannie aff a bus," it makes me laugh each time.'

Mother and son both looked at Scott as if he were talking a foreign language.

'Aye, well, maybes I'll sing it tae you baith one day – if you're really unlucky! Have you got your big bag for all the treats and money you'll get tonight Thomas?'

Thomas stretched out his hands, 'It's this big, so make sure you put lots of sweeties in mine Scott!'

88

'Don't be greedy Thomas, or I'll make Scott sing to you tonight!' laughed Wendy who loved seeing Scott and Thomas getting on so well. He was a good male role model, especially as his father had just upped and left them years ago.

'Aye, that'll serve you right loon,' joined in Scott, 'though traditionally Halloween is always the time of the year when children are allowed a bit of naughtiness, my pals used to throw eggs at the miser's doors if they wouldn't answer them or didn't give them enough sweeties.'

Wendy looked sceptical at Scott, 'I bet that was you too!'

Scott blushed, 'Aye, well, maybes aye or maybes no! Of course, we used to stretch it out to bonfire night and ask for a penny for the guy, even if we hadn't made a dummy one for the bonfire. The money sometimes went to parents to buy fireworks for the back garden. My mum and dad always took me to Aberdeen beach for the Council run fireworks display that takes place over the sea. So, I got to keep my money. Anyway, I'll be off now. I want to fit in a run before you come ringing my doorbell. I'll practice my song if you like.'

Thomas ran to Scott's side, 'Can I come too Scott?' he pleaded.

Wendy chortled, 'I'm afraid not son, Scott runs much faster than you and it is dark outside now.'

'Awwhhh,' moaned a disappointed Thomas.

Scott ran his hands over the youngster's head affectionately before putting up his palm high in the air for a high five. 'Maybe when you can reach my hand without having to jump, eh Wendy?' he asked conspiratorially.

She watched her son and Scott evade each other's palms and wished, as she often did, that she had met Scott years ago, before that poor excuse of a father Thomas had. Though she knew that Scott's heart was still broken over Naomi and a relationship was the last thing he needed. Friends they would always be, but perhaps one day she thought dreamily.

Scott unknowingly interrupted her thoughts by asking, 'Just after seven?'

'Oh, yes, try and stop him, he's looking forward to seeing which Scottish sweets you are going to give him this time!'

Scott held up his medals, 'I'll be off with these then Thomas. I'll leave you to look after the patient.'

Thomas looked forlornly at the damaged orange, but soon brightened up again, 'I can't wait to show you my new costume Scott!'

The clock tower shone brightly like a beacon upon a lighthouse guiding sailors around a hazardous coastline. Scott noted the time, a few minutes to 6pm. The old girl was keeping good time. He, like the other inhabitants of this new housing area, often wondered just who lived in the apartments below. That part of the building which also housed the workings of the clock and used to house the administration staff who ran the old CMH. He, or she, had their own private parking area and entrance. Scott had never seen anyone enter or leave and knew no-one who had either. They were a complete mystery. But he often looked up, not really for the correct time, but to see if he could see her again. The Grey Lady. Had she really gone? Sometimes there were lights on, usually of a weekend night. He wondered if it may be used as a private retreat of a busy London executive, one of those stockbroker or banker types who could afford this most expensive apartment in the complex, even during this prolonged recession. Or perhaps it was a pilot from the nearby growing Farnborough Airport. Whoever was lucky enough to earn a decent wage to pay that mortgage was the envy of Aldershot. It made his two bedroomed flat look modest. He'd heard it had several guest rooms as well as a state-of-the-art kitchen and bathroom.

He laughed as he thought of one of those yuppie types getting the fright of his life as the Grey Lady manifested in his bedroom. 'Och well,' he said aloud as he took his cue from the clock to start his warmup run. He started thinking ahead about the mile and a half of his simulated Personal Fitness Assessment, the PFA, though some of the old sweats still referred to this annual test as the BFT, the famous British Army basic or battle fitness test as some veterans still referred to it. He'd not bother doing the required sit-ups and press-ups for over two minutes for his age as he knew he could easily perform them, having done sets yesterday evening. He'd also not bother doing the lift test as he knew he could easily lift at least 20kg to the height of 1.45 metres, the equivalent of loading up to the height of an army truck. Nor would he be carrying jerry cans filled with water around 30 metres of the Wellesley estate to test his upper arms and shoulder strength. Though, maybe that would get the resident of the clock tower apartments to his or her window. Where did this nosiness come from, he now worried he was getting too urbanised. He was confident that his time in the gym would help him pass these tests. Thank goodness, he thought, that he didn't need to perform the other annual fitness test, the Basic Combat Fitness Test of an 8-mile squad run over two hours. He didn't think he was quite up to the BCFT yet and certainly wouldn't be able to complete it with his rifle and 15kg rucksack.

Scott leant against the lamppost and started stretching his calf muscles, feeling the bite and pull. After the prolonged stay in the psychiatric unit without much exercise he was glad to feel that he could now stretch for longer. He then stood up straight and began his hamstring exercises of pulling one foot behind him, bringing its heel to his buttock. He brought his knees together and pushed in his hip to maximise the stretch. He looked back up to the clock tower. 'Was it really just months ago when the fight there took place and the Grey Lady, Morag, was finally united with Hugh, her Gordon Highlander fiancée from World War One; united after a century had passed?'

He started to jog around the car park and along a row of the red bricked houses, not as striking as the granite-built houses of his home city, he thought. He passed the clock as it struck 6pm and began his run in earnest, one and a half miles where his lungs breathed in the sharp October night air, its crisp coldness hitting his lungs and coming out as warm steam clouds that puffed away like the remnants of coal smoke from a steam railway engine, his arms working like old fashioned train engine pistons to drive him faster around his timed route. He could already feel the heaviness of his leg muscles and shortness of breath; he was so out of shape. He was glad his mates at 22 Field Hospital couldn't see him now. By the time they'd be round for his late-night Halloween party, he'd be showered, washed, shaved, and changed, ready to put out a few surprises. The party was his way of saying thank you for visiting him, not judging him, and sticking by him. He knew many, like him, were still fighting their own demons, albeit more privately.

Trying to take his mind off of the pain he was subjecting his body to he thought back to history lessons in school on another Halloween day when his teacher, Mr McDonald, had taught him and his friends about the origins of this pagan celebration. He talked animatedly about the Celtic druids of seven hundred years before the birth of Christ who wanted to celebrate the end of the summer harvest whilst honouring their dead. This festival was called Samhain from the Gaelic word "samhraidhreadh" which means summer's end. His pal, Graham, had asked the teacher if he was a druid and took part in naked ceremonies too. Mr McDonald humoured Graham and said that his fellow druids found the 31st October too chilly for no clothes. He continued by telling the class that Samhain was also the name of the Celtic Lord of the Dead. The Celts thought that the dead would help their druids to make prophecies for future harvests. They lit bonfires, long before Guy Fawkes made it fashionable to do it five days later. These fires were to show the boundary where the dead should not cross so that they could not harm the living. Food would be left out to attract dead relatives and the Celts wore masks to scare off any evil spirits which is where Mr McDonald said that the custom of dressing up in costume and receiving sweets or fruit originated.

Scott ran past the two churches which made him think more of Mr McDonald who had gone on to teach them about November the 1st, All Saints' Day and November the 2nd when Ministers and Vicars would offer up prayers for the dead. He taught them that the Catholic Church in the Middle Ages wanted to introduce a Christian festival near to the pagan festival of Halloween and decided that the 1st of November would be known as All Saint's or All Hallow's Day. The night before was known as the Eve of All Hallows which many soon called Hallow Evening or Hallow Even and this was, over the years, abbreviated to Hallowe'en or Halloween. The words 'All Hallows' come from the Old English word Halig which means Holy. The 2nd of November is known as All Souls Day where the souls of the dead are honoured after the spirits and witches have flown and the Saints have been praised. It is not usually a formal holiday, but many Churches hold church services and masses where members of the congregation can meet and give prayers to dead relatives and friends. It is an important event in Mexico where the event is called the Day of the Dead. Since then Scott had seen many films that featured this macabre looking street procession, lately in James Bond, and he'd always had an urge to see it live, perhaps one day he thought.

'Jeez oh,' he breathlessly whispered to himself as he passed the barracks gates at the bottom of the route, 'I'm so unfit and struggling here.' He tried to run a bit more upright and faster because he was conscious of the armed guard watching him. He suddenly remembered about the Irishman he met in Iraq who told him that in Ireland Halloween is called Pooky Night after a mischievous spirit in Irish folklore called the púca. Scot had thought he was pulling his leg, but when he later checked on his laptop, when he finally got a connection, he found out that he was correct. He made sure he bought a drink for him the next time they met and even told him about some trivia he'd read online about England calling Halloween the Nutcrack Night or Snap Apple Night because families would eat nuts and apples in front of the fire whilst telling stories.

Scott turned back for the uphill route; he'd thought he'd saved energy for this but knew he hadn't. As he always did when he struggled in life, he thought of his dear mother, so cruelly taken from him at such a young age. He remembered going to her funeral and being given a white dove from one of his dad's friends. 'Say a prayer as you release the bird,' the man had gently said. Scott had prayed for his mother's safe delivery to Heaven as he loosened his hold on the sides of the dove. Sensing the slackened grip on its wings it flew off high into the air. Scott had watched until the white dot was no longer visible in the sky. Now he drew strength thinking how strong she was at the end, though her cancer had given her great pain. She was so worried about Scott and his father struggling without her. He ran a bit faster up the hill, drawing his anger in and thinking about why a cruel God had taken her from him and his dad. He felt guilty at blaming God, especially as he passed the two churches again, sitting in dark judgement upon his soul. He ran faster so that his guilt wouldn't surpass him. In the glare of a passing car's lights to his right he noticed a black cat run quickly across the road, narrowly missing the vehicle. It vanished into the shrubbery. 'Well that's supposed to bring me good luck, perhaps I'll get promoted to Sergeant soon,' he thought cheerfully, 'just as well it wasn't a white cat' he further reflected. They are supposed to bring bad luck if seen on this special night. If he were demoted, he'd never be able to keep his flat. He felt more guilt as he remembered benefiting from Naomi's death as her beneficiary. Her insurance had helped him put a sizeable deposit on his flat.

Soon he was back to the familiar red bricked buildings of the Wellesley estate and as he turned the corner and went up yet another, though smaller, hill he saw the familiar lights of the clock tower guiding him home like the Olympic flame to an athlete. The hill gave way to flat pavement and Scott worked his arms and legs faster, driving himself homewards. As he reached the clock tower, he could see that the time was around twelve minutes past 6pm: he was well within the 14 minutes allowed by the army for the QAs. Not quite fast enough to beat the Royal Army Medical Corps Combat Medics though; he'd have to train a bit more to beat his rivals and not have them taunting this Queen Alexandra's Royal Army Nursing Corps nurse; he had a reputation to maintain.

He gave the clock tower one more glance, he knew he wouldn't see Morag, the Grey Lady, anymore, nor Hugh, who he had briefly seen before they went away together and vanished before his very eyes. But wouldn't it just make a great Halloween if a witch went flying past the lit-up tower highlighting a black cat sitting on the broomstick. A bit clichéd he knew, but if ghosts did exist, then why can't witches? Or did they just belong in second rate ghost stories?

Water lapped over the basin as apples bobbed up and down like drowning comical jack in the boxes. Fortunately, Scott had taken the precaution of putting a plastic sheet down on the floor, a trick he had learnt from his Scout Masters. He'd enjoy watching his mates getting wet in an attempt to bob for apples, or dookin' as it was called in Scotland, after the Scots word for ducking. He'd make sure they didn't cheat by using their hands like his fellow Scouts had done. Though there were no mufflers to tie them together, he'd tell them that only their teeth could be used. This fun game also dated back to the ancient Celts who believed that Heaven would be full of apple trees packed with fruit and flowers. Scott wondered, as he always did when he heard mention of Heaven, if his mother was there and if her and Naomi had met. Was Heaven just a fantasy belief by people who wanted desperately to believe in an after-life? Hoping that one day they would be reunited with their loved ones. If not, then how to explain Naomi, Morag, and Hugh? So many unanswered questions thought Scott.

By the plastic basin Scott had thoughtfully placed several towels. No doubt some of the jokers from his Unit wouldn't be able to resist dookin the heids of those ducking for apples right into the water. He knew there would be plenty of coughing and spluttering tonight! But first he must have a shave and shower after his sweaty run.

On his way to the bathroom he lit a night candle and put it into the turnip that had taken him ages to carve over the last few nights. If folks thought carving a soft fleshed pumpkin was tough work, then they should try carving into a neep. These were traditionally used in Scotland as they were readily available at harvest time, long before pumpkins were either imported or learnt to be home grown by farmers. Two knives he had bent before he had the scary face, he was intent on. It looked even more frightening back-lit with the candle. His granny had always carved their Jack o' Lanterns and Scott now knew she must have had muscles like Hercules. Ah, but she was a wonderful woman too, his Nana, so many of his loved ones had passed over, why couldn't he see their ghosts instead, using this so-called gift from the Grey Lady. He had so much to say to them, so much left unsaid. Like many Scotsmen, he hadn't said I love you to them often enough, emotions were kept strictly under wraps in their Presbyterian household. Or at least, they were. Since losing Naomi and getting his head injury and having his father by his side during his recovery he made sure to tell him just how much he loved him whenever they parted during his leave, and how much he appreciated him.

Scott grinned at the evil looking turnip-illuminated face that stared back at him; maybe he'd not show this to Thomas, or the poor loon would have nightmares. I bet the CMT's will be more scared of this than his fellow nurses he thought wryly. These Jack o' Lanterns were originally used to scare away the evil spirits and dead people from homes. This reminded Scott of something. He went back into the kitchen, walked around the basin where the bobbing apples were still doing their aqua-dancing, and took out bottles of beer from the fridge. He leant over to the cupboard and took out bottles of Glava and Vodka. The Glava was his little taste of home, his favourite blended Scotch whisky liqueur that had been infused with spices, honey, and tangerines to give the sweetest, sharpest taste of any alcoholic drink this south of the border. Scott had more supplies that he'd bring out later, after all, he didn't want to be known as the cannie tight Aberdonian. Unlike the mean old man who was said to be the origination of the carved lanterns. This auld mannie would not entertain folk or spend his money unless he really had too. His tale tells that he was refused entry into heaven due to his meanness. His punishment was to wander with a lantern to light his way until the day of judgement. He was unable to enter Hell because of all the jokes he had played on the devil whilst alive. Though some countries think the Jack o Lanterns are faces of evil people like murderers who walk the earth revisiting the scenes of their vicious crimes. He wondered if the Wardmaster from the World War One Cambridge Military Hospital whose vision he'd seen would still be walking the clock tower for punishment of his murder. Scott liked to think that evil folk got their just rewards.

As Scott placed some of the drinks down on the refreshments table, he resisted the temptation to eat another one of the round soul cakes he had made. This tasty treat, which looked like a basic cookie, though he had put a chocolate cross across his, had been made using the recipe given to him by the Minister's wife back home in Garthdee, the area of Aberdeen where he was brought up. She still made them for the Congregation. His mum and nana used to make them too. They date back to a Christian tradition when neighbours would visit each-others houses, sing a song, and receive a soul cake. They could then pray for the soul of a deceased relative. It was the Christian Churches way of bringing Christianity to Halloween night. When Scott later received them, he would pray for his mum. When he ate one fresh from the oven this morning he prayed for his beloved Naomi.

He solemnly walked to the front door and placed some Scottish tablet on the table there. This was for Thomas, from his last visit home. It looked like traditional fudge but was crumblier and sugary with a lovely buttery aftertaste. It was made from just condensed milk, sugar, and butter. He was sure Thomas would love it; he just hoped Wendy would forgive him the high sugar content, but he knew that Thomas would already be over-excited tonight anyway. He was such a lovely laddie. Scott often wondered what the children he and Naomi would have had would have been like. He heard himself sigh and say 'Och well,' once more.

Thomas jumped up and down; the white powder from his face make-up flaked down onto the carpet like snowflakes from a teasing winter flurry. His mum looked on admiring her dab hand at miniature theatricals. She thought the red lipstick with drops going down the corners of his lips looked ever so realistic. She played along with

Thomas that Scott would faint at the sight of the blood, though she knew he'd have seen much worse. She loved her Thomas and was laughing as he swished his black cape back and forth whilst shouting, 'I want to drink your blood,' over and over again. He made a cute vampire.

'Can we go now mum; I want Scott to see me first?' he pleaded.

'No. You'll just have to learn to be patient. Scott is probably still out running. We said seven o'clock.'

'Awwhhh,' moaned a disappointed Thomas, for the second time that evening.

*****

Scott fished the spider out of the bath and brought it up to his face so that it would hear him say; 'If I was a superstitious man, I'd think that you'd be the spirit of a loved one watching over me, what with it being Halloween.' He gently put it down on the floor and watched it crawl away to the safety of the door to seek refuge. 'So, in case you are, I love you Naomi Scarlet and miss you terribly.' He watched the spider disappear. 'Och well,' he repeated as he picked up his shaving foam, squirted some out onto his fingers and started lathering it onto his face. As he absently shaved away, he looked into the mirror and caught sight of the shower rail. He'd almost forgotten! He'd need to allow time after Thomas and Wendy's visit to hang up his treacle scones. He'd also played this fun game at his Scout hut in Garthdee many years ago. He'd made a fresh batch of scones, the way his mum had taught him, this morning. He'd spread them with treacle and then tie them with a piece of thin string to the railing. Then he'd ask a guest or two to keep their hands behind their backs, lead them into the bathroom and get them to try and take a bite of the treats without using their hands. He hoped none of them would be wearing their best dresses, he was confident that the lassies wouldn't be as he'd pre-warned them, but he knew how the RAMC lads liked to dress up!

He'd planned a huge bowl of champit tatties for everyone to dive into as a communal eating feast, making sure he'd add cream and lots of butter to this mashed potato dish. He'd warn everyone to eat them carefully as he planned to add lucky charms to them. So, whoever found a coin would gain great wealth and the unlucky person who found the thimble would stay unmarried. By rights he should find it he felt because he could never marry after losing Naomi. If he'd been able to get more time off work, he would have travelled to Germany and put a candle on her grave. 'Och..' he stopped himself, he was getting in bad habits and must start thinking to the future. He eyed the shower but was drawn to the bath; just a few minutes soak he promised himself as he absently heard the noisy extraction fan finally kick in. He really must get that fixed, what a racket it made. He ran the bath, jumped in, and laid back, enjoying the warmth spreading around his body, soothing his aching legs, just a few minutes, he thought as he sleepily closed his eyes...

'It's seven o clock mummy, look,' shouted an eager Thomas, pointing to the clock on their wall.

'Well so it is my little Dracula, shall we go to Scott and...'

'Drink his blood,' interrupted Thomas, giving his best vampire impression.

'What did Thomas and Scott watch on TV when he was baby-sitting?' wondered Wendy.

'Okay Mr Vampire, let's get ready to scare Scott!'

Thomas ran to their front door, he had it opened in seconds and was already bounding across the shared landing and ringing his doorbell. 'Scott,' he shouted all a flutter, 'It's me, trick or treat,' he shouted through the letterbox. He was finally joined by his mum who handed him his treat bag which he had forgotten to pick up in his haste. He muttered a 'thanks mum,' as the door opened, and they got their surprise. Stood before them were a man and woman.

'Oh, well you're not Scott,' said an almost angry Thomas.

Wendy laughed. She thought Scott was playing a trick on them by getting two of his friends to come to his party early and surprise Thomas with their costumes.

'Why are you wearing a skirt mister,' enquired Thomas of the smiling but strangely pale man.

'It's a kilt Thomas, worn by Scotsmen like Scott, it's their national dress,' answered Wendy for the silent man. She took hold of Thomas's hand, the stirrings of uncertainty creeping into her thoughts like a cold ice cube pushed down the back of a blouse by a prankster. She involuntary shivered and hugged Thomas closer to her, not just for warmth either.

'But your top looks like an old-fashioned soldier, like in the books in Scott's flat. And so does your brown hat with the feather.' He tried to look past the man to see where Scott and his new sweets were, but a tall lady wearing a floppy white kite on her head blocked his view. Her grey dress stretched all the way to the floor, covering where her shoes should have been. He wondered if she wore big boots like the man in the skirt. 'Ooh, you've got a nice shiny medal, but Scott's got more than you,' said Thomas innocently. 'I love the colour of your short top; it almost matches my lips.' Thomas showed the lady his joke teeth.

She smiled a warm loving smile in his direction and took hold of the man's hands. Unlike Wendy, she did this in a relaxed and confident manner, as a demonstration of love and warmth. In her other hand she held up a rectangular shaped brown sweet in a clear wrapper.

'Is that for me from Scott?' asked an enthusiastic Thomas. He always buys me a sweet from Scotland. He's not going to come and sing that song about the bus and his grandmother, is he?' questioned Thomas, a little worried.

The woman and man laughed heartily. She stretched out her hand and Thomas's eager young hands gently took the Scottish tablet bar from her. He shivered as he did so.

'It looks like fudge.' He gave it an exploring sniff. 'I think I'm going to like this.' He popped it into his canvas bag with the picture of the bright orange pumpkin with the smiling face, above the words 'treats'. 'Do you two live here with Scott?' asked Thomas innocently.

Wendy shivered more violently as Morag and Hugh turned to each other, gazed lovingly at each other, turned to Wendy and in unison winked warmly to her and then bent down to Thomas's eye level and simultaneously put their fingers to their lips and said 'Shhhh.'

Author's Note

Sorry dear reader, I couldn't resist! After writing The Grey Lady Ghost of the Cambridge Military Hospital I had another visit to Aldershot to see the old CMH and I got wondering again! Would she really be able to move away after decades of caring for people? Who would be her patient?

Scott's adventures continue in The Drummer Boy, released in November 2016.

Read the first chapter of my first novel The Grey Lady Ghost of the Cambridge Military Hospital: Part 1 of the Grey and Scarlett series for free at www.cgbuswell.com where there are links to buy it in Paperback or on Kindle via Amazon.

It would help this fledgling author's career if you would please leave a review at Amazon or Good Reads or tell your friends about it using the social media links on the site or at www.facebook.com/cgbuswell and www.twitter.com/CGBUSWELL

Acknowledgements

Another big thank you to my beautiful and talented daughter, Abigail, for producing the stunning cover artwork.

The lettering and website are from the talented Richard at www.rogue.co.uk who with a few words brief always produces such creative work.

I'm indebted to 'Padre' Katherine and Ray Hyman of Cruden Bay IT Services www.crudenbaytraining.co.uk for their continuing support and proof reading. Happy Halloween guys!

Printed in Great Britain
by Amazon

22588715R00066